Ben Jonson's Catiline's Conspiracy: A Retelling

David Bruce

Published by David Bruce, 2022.

This is a work of fiction. Similarities to real people, places, or events are entirely coincidental.

BEN JONSON'S CATILINE'S CONSPIRACY: A RETELLING

First edition. July 10, 2022.

Copyright © 2022 David Bruce.

ISBN: 979-8201000660

Written by David Bruce.

Table of Contents

Source of *Catiline's Conspiracy* Cover Photo:
https://pixabay.com/photos/italy-rome-court-cicero-statue-2510287/

Educate Yourself

Read Like A Wolf Eats

Be Excellent to Each Other

Books Then, Books Now, Books Forever

In this retelling, as in all my retellings, I have tried to make the work of literature accessible to modern readers who may lack the knowledge about mythology, religion, and history that the literary work's contemporary audience had.

Do you know a language other than English? If you do, I give you permission to translate this book, copyright your translation, publish or self-publish it, and keep all the royalties for yourself. (Do give me credit, of course, for the original retelling.)

I would like to see my retellings of classic literature used in schools, so I give permission to the country of Finland (and all other countries) to give copies of any or all of my retellings to all students forever. I also give permission to the state of Texas (and all other states) to give copies of any or all of my retellings to all students forever. I also give permission to all teachers to give copies of any or all of my retellings to all students forever. Of course, libraries are welcome to use my eBooks for free.

Teachers need not actually teach my retellings. Teachers are welcome to give students copies of my eBooks as background material. For example, if they are teaching Homer's *Iliad* and *Odyssey*, teachers are welcome to give students copies of my *Virgil's* Aeneid: *A Retelling in Prose* and tell them, "Here's another ancient epic you may want to read in your spare time."

CAST OF CHARACTERS

SULLA'S GHOST. Late dictator of Rome.

CONSPIRATORS AND SUPPORTERS

LUCIUS SERGIUS **CATILINE.** Senator and Arch-conspirator. Sometimes he is called "Lucius." Sometimes he is called "Sergius." Usually he is called "Catiline."

PUBLIUS CORNELIUS **LENTULUS.** Disgraced Senator and Conspirator. In 70 B.C.E., the Censors threw LENTULUS and CURIUS out of the Senate because of LENTULUS' and CURIUS' immorality. Lentulus believes that a prophecy by the Sibyl states that he will be King of Rome. He was elected Praetor for 63 B.C.E. and was readmitted into the Senate.

CAIUS CORNELIUS **CETHEGUS.** Young Senator and Conspirator.

CURIUS. Disgraced Senator and Conspirator. In 70 B.C.E., the Censors threw LENTULUS and CURIUS out of the Senate because of LENTULUS' and CURIUS' immorality.

AUTRONIUS. Senator and Conspirator. AUTRONIUS and CORNELIUS were elected Consul-Designates for 65 B.C.E., but the election results were thrown out due to bribing of voters.

CORNELIUS. Conspirator of Equestrian Rank. Nephew to the late dictator Sulla. AUTRONIUS and CORNELIUS were elected Consul-Designates for 65 B.C.E., but the election results were thrown out due to bribing of voters.

VARGUNTEIUS. Senator and Conspirator.

LONGINUS. Senator and Conspirator. He is fat.

PORCIUS **LAECA.** Senator and Conspirator.

FULVIUS. Conspirator of Equestrian Rank.

LUCIUS **BESTIA.** Senator and Conspirator.

GABINIUS. Conspirator of Equestrian Rank. He has the epithet "Cimber," which the Gauls used for a cruel person.

STATILIUS. Conspirator of Equestrian Rank.

CEPARIUS. Supporter of Catiline.

VOLTURTIUS. Supporter of Catiline.

Note: Equestrian rank is upper class, but they are not Senators, who have the highest class.

FEMALE CHARACTERS

AURELIA ORESTILLA. Wife to Catiline. Helps recruit women to support Catiline. In this book, she is sometimes referred to as Orestilla.

FULVIA. Woman of Rank and Mistress to Curius. Informs on Catiline.

SEMPRONIA. Learnéd Noblewoman and Conspirator.

GALLA. Waiting-woman to Fulvia.

ROMAN MALE CHARACTERS, MAINLY NON-SUPPORTERS OF CATILINE

MARCUS TULLIUS **CICERO**. Consul-Elect and Later Consul for 63 B.C.E.

ANTONIUS. Consul with Cicero for 63 B.C.E.

MARCUS PORCIUS **CATO**. Righteous Senator. Grandson of Cato the Censor. Has a reputation for fairness. Also known as Cato the Younger and Cato of Utica, where he famously committed suicide following a military victory by Julius Caesar after the events of this book.

QUINTUS **CATULUS**. Elderly Senator. Enemy to Julius Caesar.

MARCUS **CRASSUS**. Wealthy Senator and Associate of Julius Caesar. After the events of the play, he became a member of the First Triumvirate with Julius Caesar and Pompey.

CAIUS JULIUS **CAESAR**. Praetor-Elect for 62 B.C.E. Pontifex Maximus for 63 B.C.E. In the play, he covertly supports Catiline, but due to political considerations, Cicero ignores this in public.

QUINTUS CICERO. Brother to Cicero.

PETREIUS. Officer. Commander of army that fights the army of Catiline.

SILANUS. Consul-Elect for 62 B.C.E.

FLACCUS. Praetor.

POMTINIUS. Praetor.

FABIUS **SANGA**. Senator and Patron of the Allobroges.

OTHER CHARACTERS

SENATORS.

ALLOBROGES. Tribesmen from Gaul who are Ambassadors who have come to Rome.

SOLDIERS.

GUARDS.
PORTER.
LICTORS.
SERVANTS.
PAGES.
CHORUS.
The SCENE: ROME.
The TIME: 63-62 B.C.E.
Before the events of the play:

In 65 B.C.E., the first Catilinarian conspiracy took place. In it, Catiline and others plotted to kill the Roman Consuls. The plot failed.

After the events of the play:

In 48 B.C.E., Julius Caesar defeats Pompey in the civil war.

In 44 B.C.E., Julius Caesar becomes *dictator perpetuo*, but he is assassinated on the Ides of March (March 15).

NOTES:

Spoiler Alert: Catiline loses. Ben Jonson's play includes a scene in which the Roman Senators decide how some of Catiline's co-conspirators will be punished.

Cicero defeated Catiline in an election to be one of the two Consuls who would rule Rome in 63 B.C.E. Catiline formed a conspiracy, and Cicero, an excellent politician as well as an excellent orator and an excellent author, thwarted it, something he boasted about in many later speeches.

At the time, and later, the Roman Republic was under attack. Later, people would accuse Julius Caesar of wanting to be crowned King of Rome. Two triumvirates — a triumvirate is a group of three powerful men — would exercise power in Rome at different times. Eventually, Octavius Caesar, the adopted son of Julius Caesar, would defeat Mark Antony and become Rome's first Emperor, ending Rome's republic.

In this play, Catiline is a villain and Cicero is a hero.

Pietas means proper, dutiful behavior. It means respect for things for which respect is due, including gods, family, and destiny. In Virgil's *Aeneid*, Aeneas is noted for his *pietas*, as when he carries his father on his back out of Troy when the city fell to the Greeks. When this book refers to piety, it is referring to this kind of dutiful behavior.

We don't read drama to learn history. In Ben Jonson's play, Catiline is thoroughly evil. In real life, he may have been thoroughly evil or may simply have had rumors spread about him. For some of his reputed evil deeds, such as committing adultery with a Vestal nun, he was found innocent in a court of law. Winston Churchill is thought to be the originator of the quotation "History is always written by the victors."

Sulla: 138–78 B.C.E.

Lucius Sergius Catiline: 108–62 B.C.E.

In this society, a person of higher rank would use "thou," "thee," and "thy" when referring to a person of lower rank. (These terms were also used affectionately and between equals.) A person of lower rank would use "you" when referring to a person of higher rank. This book uses Jonson's "thou," "thee," and "thy" only in a scene with Fulvia and Sempronia.

Roman Offices

Consuls: The office of Consul was the highest political office of the Roman Republic. Two Consuls were elected each year and served for one year. Cicero is one of the two Consuls elected early in this play.

Praetors: A Praetor can be 1) the commander of an army, or 2) a magistrate. The office of Praetor (magistrate) is the second highest political office of the Roman Republic. They were subject only to the veto of the Consuls. Praetors could take the auspices, the performance of which was a religious rite. In 63 B.C.E. Lentulus, Flaccus, and Pomtinius were Praetors. After the events of this play, Julius Caesar served as Praetor in 62 B.C.E.

Lictors: Lictors served the Consuls and carried rods and axes as symbols of the Senators' authority. Rods were symbols of the Consuls' power to inflict corporal punishment, and axes were symbols of their power to inflict capital punishment. Lictors executed punishments on those convicted.

Tribunes: Tribunes were administrative officers in Rome. Some were judicial Tribunes, and some were military Tribunes.

Aediles: An Aedile was a Roman magistrate who was in charge of maintaining public buildings. They also organized public festivals and were in charge of weights and measures.

Censors: They supervised public morality and maintained the census.

Prefects: They had civil or military power, but that power was delegated to them from others.

CHAPTER 1

— 1.1 —

The ghost of Sulla, a deceased dictator of Rome, appeared. The year was 63 B.C.E., and he had been dead for 15 years. The first Roman civil war pitted Sulla versus Marius. Sulla won. As dictator, in 81 B.C.E. Sulla condemned many people to death by putting their names on proscription lists. The young Catiline had fought under him.

Sulla's Ghost now prophesied the destruction of Rome and urged Catiline to be cruel and commit the evilest deeds:

"Don't you feel me, Rome? Not yet? Is night so heavy on you, and my weight so light?

"Can Sulla's Ghost arise within your walls and be regarded as less than an earthquake threatening the imminent destruction of you and yours?"

Sulla's Ghost continued:

"Don't the frightened heads of your lofty towers shake? Don't they shrink to their very foundations?

"Won't the collapse of your lofty towers fill the large Tiber River and make the river swell up and drown the seven proud hills that you are built on?

"What sleep is this that seizes you, a sleep so like death and yet is not death? Wake, and feel her — feel death — in my breath.

"Behold, I come, sent from the Stygian sound — the River Styx — like a poisonous dire vapor that had cleft the ground to mix with the night and blight the day, or like a pestilence that would display and spread infection through the world — which, thus, I do."

He pointed to the infection: Catiline, who was in his study.

Sulla's Ghost continued:

"May Pluto, god of the Land of the Dead, be present at your — Catiline's — deliberations; and let Sulla's spirit enter into your darker bosom. All that was mine, and bad, let your breast inherit.

"Alas, how weak is that, for Catiline!

"Did I but say — vain voice! — all that was mine?

"All that the Gracchi, Cinna, Marius — revolutionaries all — would; and what now, if I — coming from hell — had a body again, I could; what fiends would wish would be; and worse than Hannibal the Carthaginian general who brought elephants across the Alps to attack Rome could have wished to see, I wish you, Catiline, to think and carry out."

The Gracchi were two brothers who instituted land and social reforms; they were opposed by the conservative Senators and were murdered separately, in 133 and 121 B.C.E. Some people may think that the reforms of the Gracchi were justified; Sulla does not.

During Sulla's absence from Rome, Cinna and Marius wreaked vengeance on Roman aristocrats.

Hannibal terrified Roman citizens in the Second Punic War.

Sulla's Ghost was wishing for Catiline to be as revolutionary as the Gracchi, as vengeful as Cinna and Marius, as fiendish as fiends, and to terrify Roman citizens worse than Hannibal could have wished to do.

Sulla's Ghost continued:

"Let the long-hid seeds of treason in you now shoot forth in evil deeds ranker than horror, and your former evil crimes not be mentioned except to urge the doing of new evil acts.

"Let your consciousness of your former crimes provoke you on to commit more crimes.

"Let your incests, murders, and rapes be always in your mind.

"Let your raping first a Vestal nun be always in your mind."

The Vestal nun was Fabia, the half-sister of Cicero's wife: Terentia.

Vestal nuns were virgins who attended on Vesta, goddess of the hearth.

Sulla's Ghost continued:

"Let your parricide, recently, on your own only son, be always in your mind after his mother, to make empty way for your most recent wicked nuptials, be always in your mind."

In this culture, "parricide" referred to the murder of a close relative, who was not necessarily a father. Catiline murdered his first wife and his son in order to be able to marry his second wife, who was wealthy and beautiful and did not wish to have an adult stepson.

Sulla's Ghost continued:

"Worse than those crimes is that blazing, flagrant crime, that act of your incestuous life, which got you at once a daughter and a wife."

Catiline had committed incest with his own daughter.

Sulla's Ghost continued:

"I pass over and don't mention the slaughters that you did for me, of Senators, for which I hid for you your murder of your brother, being so bribed, and wrote him in the list of my proscribed after your evil deed, to save your little shame."

Catiline was accused of murdering people for Sulla after Sulla made up his lists of proscriptions. These were lists of people whom Sulla regarded as enemies of the state. They were murdered, and their property was confiscated. Catiline murdered his own brother-in-law. After the murder, the brother-in-law's name was added to a list of proscriptions, making the murder legal.

Sulla's Ghost continued:

"Your incest with your sister I do not name.

"All of these crimes I have mentioned are too slight and trivial.

"Fate will have you pursue new evil deeds after which no evil can be new: The new evil deeds will result in the ruin of your country.

"You were built for such a work, and you were born for no less guilt.

"So what if you were defeated once before, and your plot was discovered? Attempt now to overthrow your country once again."

Catiline had been involved in a conspiracy to murder Roman Consuls and Senators two years earlier in 65 B.C.E.

Sulla's Ghost continued:

"The ruin of Rome is your act, or none.

"What all the several evils that visit earth, brought forth by night with a sinister birth — what plagues, famine, fire — and what the sword and sicknesses of excess, could not achieve, let your fury do."

In this society, night air was regarded as dangerous.

Sulla's Ghost continued:

"Make all past, present, future evil your own, and conquer all example — outdo all previous similar crimes and evils — in your own singular example.

"Nor let your thought find any vacant time to hate an old crime, but always let a fresher crime drown the remembrance of the old crime.

"Don't let evil cease, but while it is in the act of punishing, let it increase.

"Let conscience and care — worry and caution — die in you and let not even heaven itself be free from your impiety — your neglect of your duty to gods and men.

"Let night grow blacker with your plots, and let day, at the showing of just your head forth, start away from this half-sphere (the half of the world illuminated by the sun), and leave Rome's blinded — deprived of light — walls to embrace lusts, hatreds, slaughters, funerals, and not recover sight until their own flames light them to their ruins.

"Let all the names of your confederates, too, be no less great in Hell than here, so that when we would repeat our strengths in a roll-call of names, we may name you all."

In Dante's *Inferno*, the sinners in the lower circles of Hell do not wish to give Dante the Pilgrim their names because they do not want to be remembered in the Land of the Living.

Sulla's Ghost continued:

"And let Furies call upon you for Furies, while what you do may strike them into fears, or make them grieve and wish your evil deeds theirs."

Sulla was saying that he wanted Catiline and his co-conspirators to become more dreadful than the Furies: avenging goddesses of Hell. He wanted Catiline and his co-conspirators to strike fear into the Furies or to make the Furies grieve because Catiline and his co-conspirators did more fearsome deeds than they — the Furies — did.

Sulla's Ghost exited.

Catiline had been unable to hear the words that Sulla's Ghost had spoken, although those words had echoed some of his own thoughts.

Alone in his study, Catiline spoke:

"It is decided; I know what I shall do. Nor shall your fate, Rome, resist my vow. Though hills were set on hills and seas met seas to guard you, I would win through."

The giants Otus and Ephialtes wanted to pile mountain on mountain to attack — not protect — the gods. These two giants made war against the gods and attempted to carry away goddesses to make them their wives. Otus wanted to marry Diana, and Ephialtes wanted to marry Juno. Part of their plan was to pile the mountains Ossa and Pelion on top of Mount Olympus. The Olympian gods defeated the two giants.

The steep Alps help protect northern Italy from invasions.

The Tyrrhenian Sea, the Ionian Sea, and the Adriatic Sea help guard Italy.

Catiline continued:

"Aye, plow up rocks, steep as the Alps, in dust and dip up the Tyrrhenian Sea waters into clouds, but I would reach your head, proud city.

"The evils that I have done cannot be made safe and secure from reprisal except by greater attempts to do greater evils; and I feel a spirit within me that chides my sluggish hands and says they have been innocent and have not been doing harm for too long."

An attempt is a dangerous undertaking, such as an assault or attack.

Catiline continued:

"Was I a man bred great as Rome herself? One formed for all her honors, all her glories, equal to all her titles? A man who could stand close up with Atlas, and sustain Rome's name as strongly as Atlas holds up heaven on his shoulders?"

Atlas was a Titan — a pre-Olympian god — who was condemned to hold up the sky for eternity after the Titans lost a war against the Olympian gods.

Catiline continued:

"And was I, of all Rome's brood, marked out for the repulse — defeat in the election — by Rome's no-voice, no-vote, and rejection, when I stood as a candidate to be commander in the Pontic War?"

The Roman general Pompey defeated King Mithridates VI, King of Pontus, in the Third Mithridatic War. Catiline resented not being given command of the Roman forces.

Catiline continued:

"I will hereafter call Rome my stepdame and no true mother, forever. If she can lose her nature, I can lose my piety, and in her stony entrails I will dig me a seat where I will live again as the labor of her womb, and I will be a burden weightier than all the prodigies and monsters that she has been pregnant with and given birth to since she first knew Mars."

According to Catiline, Rome has treated him badly and so he will make her give birth to him as a monster worse than all the other monsters she has given birth to.

Mars, the Roman god of war, was the father of Romulus and Remus, twin brothers who founded Rome. Their mother was Rhea Silva.

Aurelia, Catiline's wife, entered the study.

"Who's there?" Catiline asked.

"It is I," Aurelia answered.

"Aurelia?"

"Yes."

"Appear," Catiline said, "and break like day, my beauty, to this circle — this orb, this world. Upbraid your sun-god Phoebus Apollo because he is so long in mounting to that summit that should give you your proper splendor."

The name "Aurelia" is derived from the Latin word *aureus*, which means "golden."

"Why does my sweetheart frown?" Catiline asked. "Have I too long been absent from these lips, this cheek, these eyes?"

He kissed them.

"What is my trespass?" Catiline said. "Speak."

"It seems you know what your trespass is, you who can accuse yourself," Aurelia answered.

In fact, he had too long been absent from her lips, her cheek, her eyes.

"I will redeem it," Catiline promised.

"Always you say you will," Aurelia Orestilla responded. "But when?"

Catiline answered, "When Orestilla, by bearing well these my retirements and stolen times for thought, shall give their effects permission to call her Queen of all the world, in place of humbled Rome."

Catiline was plotting to become King of Rome. That was the reason for his retirements and stolen times for thought. When he and Aurelia became King and Queen of Rome, there would be no need for these retirements and stolen times for thought, he believed.

"You court me now," Aurelia said.

He wanted to put her in a royal court, and he was courting — persuading — her to act the way he wanted her to act.

"As I would always, love, by this ambrosiac kiss" — he kissed her — "and" — he kissed her a second time — "this kiss of nectar."

Ambrosia is the food of the gods, and nectar is the drink of the gods.

Catiline continued:

"If you would only hear as gladly as I speak. Could my Aurelia think I meant her less when, wooing her, I first removed a wife and then a son in order to make my bed and house spacious and fit to embrace her?"

He was referring to his murdering his first wife and then his son so that he could marry Aurelia, his second wife.

Catiline continued:

"These were deeds not to have begun with but to end with more and greater. He who, building, stops at one floor, or the second, has erected nothing.

"I was meditating on how to raise you and make you Queen of Rome. I was meditating on how to make some act of mine answer your love, that love which, when my state was now quite sunk, came with your wealth and raised it up again."

Aurelia's wealth had allowed Catiline to pay off his debts.

Catiline continued:

"Your love that also made my arising fortune once more look above the main, above the high sea, which now shall hit the stars and stick my Orestilla there, among them, if any tempest can but make the billow, and any billow can but lift her greatness."

Heroes and great personages are found among the stars in constellations such as those named after Orion the Hunter, Hercules, and Perseus.

Catiline continued:

"But I must pray to my love that she will put on like habits with myself and act as I do. I have to do with many men and many natures."

Catiline was skilled at manipulating people. He wanted her to also manipulate people.

The word "habits" meant 1) clothes, and 2) habitual practice. Catiline wanted his wife, like him, to dress and act a part in order to manipulate people.

Catiline continued:

"Some men must be blown — puffed up — and soothed, such as Lentulus, whom I have exalted with exaggerating his noble blood and family and with a vain dream out of the Sibyl's books of prophecy."

Sibyls are female prophets.

Before Rome became a republic, an old woman — the Cumaean Sibyl in disguise — arrived in Rome and offered to sell to King Tarquin — Lucius

Tarquinius Superbus, the last Roman king — nine books of prophecy at a high price. When he declined to buy them, the Sibyl burned three books and then offered to sell to him the remaining six books at the same high price. When he declined to buy them, the Sibyl burned three more books and then offered to sell to him the remaining three books at the same high price. He bought them.

Catiline continued:

"The vain dream is that a third man of that great family whereof he is descended, the Cornelii, should be a king in Rome — which I have hired the flattering augurs to interpret the third man as being him, Cinna and Sulla being dead."

According to these fortune-tellers, the three Cornelii were Cinna, Sulla, and Lentulus. One of these men was supposed to become King of Rome, and Cinna and Sulla were dead. In fact, Catiline had bribed the augurs to interpret the Sibylline prophecies in this way.

Catiline continued:

"Then, there is bold Cethegus, whose valor I have turned into his poison and praised him so into daring that when I would bid him move, he would make an attack upon the gods, kiss lightning, wrest the thunderbolt away from the Cyclops, and fire the thunderbolt directly at the face of a full, swelling cloud, and resist his — Jove's — anger."

The one-eyed Cyclops made thunderbolts for Jupiter, king of gods and men, to use.

Catiline continued:

"Others there are whom malice to the state attracts and incites for contumelies — contemptuous treatment — received; and such are sure ones, such as Curius and the forenamed Lentulus, both of whom have been degraded in the Senate."

In 70 B.C.E., the Censors threw Lentulus and Curius out of the Senate because of Lentulus' and Curius' immorality.

Catiline continued:

"And both must have their disgraces always newly rubbed — the disgraces are like a sore — to make them smart, and labor for revenge.

"Others are there whom mere ambition fires. They have vainly convinced themselves that they have a chance to achieve the governorship of provinces abroad, and I have promised the provinces to them.

"These men include Laeca, Vargunteius, Bestia, and Autronius.

"Some there are whom their needs oppress, such as the idle, unemployed captains of Sulla's troops; and diverse Roman knights, the profuse wasters of their patrimonies, who are so threatened by their debts that they will now take any desperate risk for a change.

"These for a time we must relieve and assist, Aurelia, and make our house their safeguard and protection; we must do that for those who fear the law, or stand within her control, for any act past or to come.

"Such men will be seditious because of their own crimes, as they will be from our crimes.

"Some more men there are, who are slight airlings — rash youngsters — and who will be won with the gifts of dogs, and horses, or perhaps a whore — which must be had.

"And if they risk their lives for us, Aurelia, we must risk our honors a little.

"Get a quantity and a variety of women, as I have gotten of boys; and give them time and place and every encouragement to sin."

Some of the conspirators would be bribed with prostitutes, both female and male.

Catiline continued:

"You yourself, too, shall be courtly and be courtly flattering, and entertain, and feast, stay up late, and revel. Call all the great, the fair, and the spirited dames of Rome about you, and begin a fashion of freedom and social intercourse and licentiousness.

"Some will thank you, although the sour Senators frown, whose heads must ache in fear and feeling — and presentiment, too."

The heads could ache because of the growing of the invisible horns that cuckolds — men with unfaithful wives — wore. Or the heads could ache because they were beaten.

Catiline continued:

"We must not spare either expense or modesty. It can but show like one of Juno's or one of Jove's disguises in either you or me; and will as soon, when things succeed, be thrown aside or let fall as is a veil put off, a mask changed, or the scene — a place of dramatic action — shifted in our theaters —"

The gods, such as Jupiter — Jove — and his wife, Juno, could assume disguises, pretending to be mortal humans, for example. When the need for the disguise was over, they would appear as their true immortal selves.

Catiline was interrupted by a noise outside the room.

"Who's that?" he said. "It is the voice of Lentulus."

"Or of Cethegus," Aurelia said.

"Go into another room, my fair Aurelia, and think upon these stratagems," Catiline said. "They must not see how far you are trusted with these secret matters, although you rise on their shoulders, necks, and heads."

The rebellion of these men could make Aurelia the Queen of Rome.

Aurelia exited the room from one door.

Lentulus and Cethegus entered from another door.

Lentulus was a disgraced Senator who hoped to become King of Rome because of a supposed prophecy by the Cumaean Sibyl, and Cethegus was a young Senator.

"It is, I think, a morning full of fate!" Lentulus said. "Dawn rises slowly, as if her sullen car — her gloomy, sluggish chariot — had all the weights of sleep and death hung at it."

In Roman mythology, the goddess Dawn arrives in a chariot pulled by two horses.

Lentulus continued, "Dawn is not rosy fingered but swollen black. Her face is like a water turned to blood, and her sick head is bound about with clouds, as if she threatened night before the noon of day. This dawn does not look as if it would have a 'hail' or 'health' wished in it, as on other morns."

"Hail" is a Roman greeting.

Cethegus said, "Why, all the fitter, Lentulus: Our coming is not for salutation; we have business to conduct."

"Nobly said, brave Cethegus," Catiline said.

Then he asked, "Where's Autronius?"

"Hasn't he come?" Cethegus asked.

"He is not here," Catiline said.

"Hasn't Vargunteius come?" Cethegus asked.

"No," Catiline answered.

Cethegus said, "Let a fire be in their beds and bosoms, who so will serve their sloth rather than virtue and courage! They are no Romans, not when they act so lethargically at such a time of high need as now."

Lentulus said, "Both Autronius and Vargunteius, as well as Longinus, Laeca, Curius, Fulvius, and Gabinius, gave me the word last night, by Lucius Bestia, that they would all be here, and early."

"They did?" Cethegus said. "As you would have overslept, had I not called you. Come, we all sleep and are mere sleepy dormice, flies little less than dead; more dullness hangs on us than on the morn. We're spirit-bound in ribs — bars — of ice; our whole bloods are one stone; and honor cannot thaw us, nor our wants, although they burn hot as fevers to our states of being."

"I wonder why they would be tardy at an hour of so great purpose and importance," Catiline said.

Cethegus said:

"If the gods had called them to a purpose, they would just have come with the same tortoise speed, they who are thus slow to have come to such an action, which the gods will envy, as asking no less means than all their powers conjoined to effect.

"I would have seen Rome burnt by this time, and her ashes in an urn, the kingdom of the Senate rent asunder, and the degenerate talking gown run frightened out of the air of Italy."

The degenerate talking gown is Cicero, the orator who, like other Roman citizens, wore a toga during formal occasions.

"Spirit of men!" Catiline said, praising Cethegus. "You heart of our great enterprise! How much I love these voices — these opinions and expressions of emotion — in you!

Cethegus said, "Oh, for the days of Sulla's sway, when the free sword took leave to act all that it would!"

Catiline added, "And the sword was as familiar with entrails as our augurs!"

Augurs sacrificed animals and examined their entrails as a way of divining the future. Sulla's supporters were as familiar with the entrails of humans as augurs were with the entrails of animals.

Cethegus said, "Sons killed fathers. Brothers killed their brothers."

Catiline added, "And they received price — high esteem — and praise for acting in such a way. All hate had license given to it, and all rage was given the reins so it could run unchecked."

Cethegus said, "Slaughter straddled the streets and stretched himself to seem huger, while to his stained thighs the gore he drew flowed up and carried down whole heaps of limbs and bodies through the arch made by Slaughter's legs. No age was spared, and neither sex was spared."

"None, and no rank in society," Catiline said.

"Infants in the entrance of life were not free from slaughter," Cethegus said. "The sick, the old, who could hope for only a day longer to live by the natural order of things, were not allowed to stay that extra day in the Land of the Living. Virgins and widows, matrons, pregnant wives — all died."

"It was crime enough that they had lives," Catiline said.

To Catiline, the fact that these people were alive was reason enough to kill them.

He continued, "To strike but only those who could do hurt was dull, and poor. Some fell to make the number, as some fell to make the prey, aka the booty."

Some died simply to increase the number of the dead; others died because they had possessions that could be looted.

Cethegus said, "The rugged Charon fainted, and asked for a navy, rather than a boat, to ferry the newly dead over the river Styx to the sad, sorry, heavy world that is the Land of the Dead."

Charon was a ferryman who transported the souls of the dead across a river to Hades, the Land of the Dead. So many people died in Sulla's civil war that Charon needed an entire navy rather than a single ferry to transport the souls of the dead.

Cethegus continued, "The maws — stomachs — and dens of beasts could not receive the bodies that those souls were frighted from; and even the graves were filled with men yet living, whose flight and fear had mixed them with the dead."

"And this shall be again, and more, and more," Catiline said, "now that Lentulus, the third Cornelius, is to stand up and be eminent in Rome."

"Nay, don't urge that which is so uncertain," Lentulus said.

"What do you mean?" Catiline said.

"I mean, not cleared and proven to be trustworthy, and therefore not to be reflected on," Lentulus said.

"The Sibyl's leaves uncertain?" Catiline said. "Or the comments of our grave, deep, divining men not clear?"

The Cumaean Sibyl wrote her prophecies on leaves.

The augurs interpreted those prophecies.

"All prophecies, you know, suffer the torture," Lentulus said.

Roman slaves and foreigners were tortured to extract confessions or testimony.

Prophecies tend to be uncertain and unclear. Many meanings can be tortured — interpreted — out of them.

"But this prophecy already has confessed without torture," Catiline said, "and it has been so weighed, examined, and set forth that it would be malicious ignorance in that man who would be faint in the belief."

According to Catiline, the prophecy that Lentulus would be King of Rome was completely clear.

"Do you believe it?" Lentulus asked.

"Do I love Lentulus?" Catiline asked. "Or pray to see him become King of Rome?"

"The augurs all are in agreement in saying that I am the member of the Cornelius family meant to be King of Rome," Lentulus said.

The augurs — whom Catiline had bribed — all said that the prophecy stated that Lentulus would be king.

"They would have shown that they had lost their science of augury if they were not in agreement," Catiline said.

"They count from Cinna," Lentulus said.

Lucius Cornelius Cinna had been a four-time Consul of Rome.

"And Sulla next, and so that makes you the third, and the third shall be king," Catiline said. "All who can say the sun has risen must think it."

Lentulus' becoming king soon was as obvious as the newly risen sun. So said Catiline.

"Men notice me more recently, as I come forth," Lentulus said.

Catiline said:

"Why, what can they do less? Cinna and Sulla are set like the sun, and they are gone; and we must turn our eyes on him who is, and shines.

"Noble Cethegus, just view him with me, here! He looks already as if he shook a scepter over the Senate and the awed purple dropped their rods and axes!"

Roman Senators wore a tunic or a toga with a purple stripe, and their Lictors carried rods and axes as symbols of the Senators' authority. Rods were symbols of their power to inflict corporal punishment, and axes were symbols of their power to inflict capital punishment.

Catiline continued, "The statues melt again."

In 65 B.C.E., lightning struck the Capitol and melted statues — a foreboding omen.

Catiline continued, "And household gods in groans confess the travail of the city."

When Troy fell, the greatest Trojan warrior, Hector, who was carrying the image of Vesta, goddess of the hearth, appeared before Aeneas in a dream and told him to leave the burning city and to rescue the city's household gods. Later, the household gods appeared to Aeneas in a dream and told him to go to Italy, where Aeneas became an important ancestor of the Romans.

Catiline continued, "The very walls sweat blood before the change; and stones start out to ruin, before the change comes."

"But he, and we, and all are idle still," Cethegus said.

"I am your obedient follower, Sergius," Lentulus said.

Catiline's full name was Lucius Sergius Catiline.

Lentulus continued, "And whatever the great Cornelian name shall succeed in becoming, it is not augury, nor the Sibyl's books, but Catiline who makes it."

"I am the shadow to honored Lentulus and Cethegus here, who are the heirs of Mars," Catiline said.

Cethegus praised Catiline by saying, "By Mars himself, I say that Catiline is more my parent, for whose virtue Earth cannot make a shadow great enough, although envy should come, too."

Others were heard approaching.

"Oh, there they are," Cethegus said. "Now we shall talk more, although we yet do nothing."

Autronius, Vargunteius, Longinus, Curius, Laeca, Bestia, Fulvius, Gabinius, and some servants entered Lucius Sergius Catiline's study.

"Hail, Lucius Catiline," Autronius said.

"Hail, noble Sergius," Vargunteius said to Catiline.

"Hail, Publius Lentulus," Longinus said.

"Hail, the third Cornelius," Longinus said to Lentulus.

"Caius Cethegus, hail," Laeca said.

"Hail, sloth and words, instead of men and spirits," Cethegus said to everyone.

Trying to keep the peace, Catiline said, "Nay, dear Caius —"

"Are your eyes unseeled yet?" Caius Cethegus said. "Are your eyes still blinded?"

A young falcon's eyes were stitched closed — seeled — during its early training. After its training, the falcon's stitches were removed.

Cethegus continued, "Dare they look at even a dull day?"

Catiline said, "He's zealous for the affair concerning which you have come, and he blames you for your tardy coming, gentlemen."

Cethegus began, "Unless we had sold ourselves to sleep and ease, and would be our slaves' slaves —"

Trying to keep the peace, Catiline interrupted, "— please don't criticize them."

Cethegus began, "The north is not so stark and cold —"

Catiline interrupted, "— Cethegus —"

"We shall redeem all, if your fire will let us," Bestia said.

"You are too full of lightning, noble Caius," Catiline said to Cethegus.

He then said to a servant, "Boy, see that all the doors are shut so that no one approaches us in this part of the house."

He then ordered another servant, "Go and tell the priest to kill the slave I designated last night and tell him to bring me some of the slave's blood when I shall call for him.

"Until then, all you servants wait outside."

The servants exited.

Darkness appeared and covered the scene. It was an omen.

"What is it, Autronius?" Vargunteius asked.

"Longinus?" Autronius asked.

"Curius?" Longinus asked.

"Laeca?" Curius asked.

"Do you feel nothing?" Vargunteius asked.

"A strange unwonted horror invades me," Longinus said. "I don't know what it is. A darkness comes over the place."

"The day goes back," Laeca said. "Or else my senses do."

"As at Atreus' feast!" Curius said.

Atreus and Thyestes were brothers, but Thyestes committed adultery with Atreus' wife and through trickery took Atreus' crown as King of Mycenae. To get revenge, Atreus killed Thyestes' three sons and cooked them, except for their hands and feet. After Thyestes had eaten the flesh of his sons, Atreus showed him their hands and feet, which Thyestes recognized. In horror at the deed, the gods caused darkness.

"Darkness grows more and more!" Fulvius said.

"The vestal flame on the altar in Vesta's shrine in the Roman Forum, I think, has gone out," Lentulus said.

This was indeed an ominous sign.

A groan of many people sounded from underground.

Hades, the Land of the Dead, is located underground.

"What groan was that?" Gabinius asked.

"It comes from our imaginations," Cethegus said. "Let us strike fire out of ourselves and force a day. We can provide light through our own fieriness."

One way to create fire is by striking flint against metal.

Another groan sounded from underground.

"Again it sounds!" Autronius said.

"As if all the city gave it!" Bestia said.

"We fear what we ourselves imagine," Cethegus said.

A fiery light appeared.

"What light is this?" Vargunteius asked.

"Look out the window!" Curius said.

"It still grows greater," Lentulus said.

"From where does it come?" Laeca asked.

"It is a bloody arm that holds a pine torch lighted above the Capitol," Longinus said, looking out the window. "And now it waves to us!"

"Splendid and full of omen!" Catiline said. "Our enterprise is sealed and confirmed."

He interpreted the omen as propitious to their rebellion.

"In spite of darkness that would look with disfavor on it," Cethegus said. "Look no more. We lose time and ourselves to what we came for. Speak, Lucius! We will pay attention to you."

They were losing time by looking at the omens; although Cethegus did not know it, they were losing themselves by rebelling against the Roman Republic.

Lucius Sergius Catiline said:

"Noblest Romans, if you were less, or if your faith and virtue did not justify that title of Roman as does your blood and birth, I should not now unprofitably spend myself in words or snatch at empty hopes, by airy ways, for solid certainties."

In other words, if those present had not shown themselves to be good Romans, Catiline would not now be speaking and forming plans, which would be uncertain (because not backed by good Romans) to achieve solid certainties: victory in their rebellion.

In his speech, Catiline was assuming both that the co-conspirators were good Romans and that the rebellion would succeed.

Catiline continued:

"But because in many, and the greatest, dangers, I always have known you to be no less true than valiant, and because I perceive in you the same inclinations to want or not want, to think things good or bad, alike with me — which testifies to and gives evidence of your firm friendship — I dare the more boldly to set out on foot with you or to lead to this great and goodliest — most splendid — action.

"What I have thought of it before, you all have heard individually. I then expressed my zeal to the glory. Now the need inflames me, when I consider beforehand the hard conditions that our states of condition must undergo, unless in due course we redeem ourselves to liberty and break the iron yoke forged for our necks.

"For, what less can we call it, when we see the commonwealth so monopolized by a few, the giants of the state, who by turns enjoy her and defile her? All the earth, her kings and petty rulers, are their tributaries — rulers who pay tribute. People and nations pay them hourly taxes and tribute money. The riches of the world flow to their coffers, and not to Rome's.

"While, except for those few, the rest, however great we are, however honest and valiant, are herded with the common people, and so kept as if we were bred only to consume grain, or wear out wool, to drink the city's water, to be without honors, without authority or distinction, trembling beneath their rods, to whom, if all were well in Rome, we should come forth like bright axes and be feared."

According to Catiline, only a very few people in Rome enjoyed wealth and high rank. In contrast, Catiline and his co-conspirators, although deserving of wealth and high rank, were treated like mere consumers and common people. The great Romans wanted Catiline and his co-conspirators to fear their rod, but Catiline wanted himself and his co-conspirators to attack the great men of Rome with axes.

Catiline continued:

"All places, honors and magistracies, and high offices are theirs, or they are where they will confer them! They leave us the dangers and liability, the repulses, the judgments and decreed obligations, the lacks and wants, which how long will you bear, most valiant spirits?

"Wouldn't we be better off to fall, once, with virtue than draw a wretched and dishonored breath, to lose with shame, when these men's pride will laugh?

"I call the faith of gods and men as witness: The power is in our hands, our bodies are able, and our minds are as strong as our bodies. In contrast, in them all things have grown aged and decayed with their wealth and years.

"There lacks but only to begin the business. The outcome of our rebellion is certain."

"On, let us go on," Cethegus and Longinus said.

"Go on, brave Sergius," Curius and Bestia said.

Lucius Sergius Catiline continued:

"It strikes my soul — and who can escape that stroke, whoever has a soul or just the smallest breath of man within him? — to see them swell with treasure, which they pour out in their riots, eating, drinking, building. Yes, building, in the sea, planing and making level of hills with valleys, and raising valleys above hills, while we lack the necessities to give to our bodies.

"They have their multiple houses, manors, lordships. We scarcely have a fire or a poor household god — a Lar!"

Actually, Catiline and the co-conspirators were members of the Roman upper class.

Catiline continued:

"They buy rare Attic statues, Tyrian hangings, Ephesian pictures, and Corinthian plate, Attalic garments, and now newly found gems since Pompey went for Asia. These things they purchase at the price of provinces.

"The river Phasis cannot afford them fowl nor can Lucrine Lake afford them oysters enough; Mount Circeo, too, is searched to please the ingenious gluttony of a meal!"

The wealthy of Rome were feasting so much that Italy could not supply them with sufficient quantities of delicacies.

Catiline continued:

"Their ancient habitations they neglect and set up new habitations; then, if the echo is not pleasing in such a room, they pluck down those and build newer, alter them, too; and by all frantic ways they vex and keep in constant use their wild wealth, as they molest the people from whom they forcibly grab it.

"Yet, they cannot tame or overcome or exhaust their riches: not by making baths, orchards, fish-pools, letting in of seas here, and then there forcing them out again with mountainous heaps, for which the earth has lost most of her ribs — strata of rock — as entrails, being now wounded no less for marble than for gold.

"We all this while, like calm, benumbed spectators, sit until our residences do crack, and we do not hear the thundering ruins, while at home our needs, abroad our debts, subject us to pressure, our states of condition daily tending to bad, our hopes to worse; and what is left but for us to be crushed?

"Wake, wake, brave friends, and meet the liberty you often have wished for! Behold: Renown, riches, and glory court you. Fortune holds out these to you as rewards.

"I think, even if I were silent and unable to speak, the affair itself, the opportunity, your needs and dangers, with the splendid spoil the war brings, should invite you.

"Treat me as your general or your soldier. Neither my mind nor my body shall be lacking to you. And, once being newly elected Consul, I do not fear to do and effect all that you wish, as long as your trust in me does not flatter and blind me, and as long as you'd not rather still be slaves than be free."

"Free! Free!" Cethegus said.

"It is freedom we choose!" Longinus said.

"It is freedom we all stand for!" Curius said.

"Why, these are noble voices!" Catiline said. "Nothing is lacking, then, but that we take a solemn oath to strengthen our commitment to our plot."

"And so to act it," Cethegus said. "Deferring and delaying hurts, where powers are so prepared."

The word "powers" can mean 1) strengths, and 2) troops.

Autronius said, "Yet, before we enter into open act of rebellion — with your permission — it would be no loss, if it might be enquired what the condition of these arms would be?"

Autronius, who had been involved two years earlier in the first Catilinarian conspiracy, which failed, was rightly concerned about things that might stop this new conspiracy from succeeding.

"Aye, and the means to carry us through?" Vargunteius said.

Catiline said, "What, friends! Do you think that I would ask you to grasp the wind? Or call you to the embracing of a cloud?"

Ixion tried to rape the goddess Juno, but her husband, Jupiter, king of the gods, foiled the attempt by making a cloud take on the appearance of Juno. Punished in Hades, Ixion is bound on a flaming wheel that constantly spins.

Catiline continued:

"Do you think I would risk your recognized valors — your worth and valor — in so dear a business and have no other second — support and assistance — than the danger, nor any other garland than the loss? Become your own assurances and guarantees.

"And, for the means, consider, first, the stark safety — the absolute feeling of security from danger — the commonwealth is in now. The whole Senate is sleepy and is dreaming about no such violent blow.

"Their forces — armies — are all abroad, of which the greatest, which might annoy us most, is farthest off, in Asia under the command of Pompey. Those forces that are near at hand are commanded by our friends. One army in Spain is commanded by Gnaeus Piso; the other army in Mauritania is commanded by Nucerinus. Both of these generals I have firm and fast — they are committed to helping us in our plot.

"I myself, then, am standing as a candidate now to be Consul, with my hoped-for colleague Caius Antonius, one who is no less engaged and committed to our cause by his wants and needs than we are, and whom I have the power to melt and cast in any mold."

Catiline was saying that he could manipulate Caius Antonius, who was also campaigning to be one of the two Consuls for the next year.

Catiline continued:

"Besides these men, there are some others who will not yet be named, both sure and great ones, who, when the time comes, shall declare themselves strong for our party; so that no resistance in nature — that is, anywhere — can be thought.

"As for our reward after our victory, then:

"First, all our debts are paid.

"The dangers of law, actions, decrees, judgments against us are acquitted.

"The rich men, as in Sulla's times, are proscribed, and confiscation made of all their goods."

Catiline pointed to various co-conspirators as he said, continuing to use the present tense:

"That house is yours; that land is his; those waters, orchards, and walks are a third's. He has that honor, and he has that office. Such a province falls to Vargunteius, this province falls to Autronius, that province falls to bold Cethegus, Rome falls to Lentulus.

"You share the world, her magistracies, priesthoods, wealth, and felicity among yourselves, friends, and Catiline is your servant.

"Would you, Curius, revenge the contumely and disgrace stuck upon you in being removed from the Senate? Now, now is your time to do so.

"Would Publius Lentulus strike blows for the like disgrace? Now is his time.

"Would stout and bold Longinus walk the streets of Rome, openly opposing and defying the important person who holds the powerful office of Praetor? Now has he a time to spurn and tread the fasces — bundles of rods and a single-headed ax — into dirt made of the usurers' and the Lictors' brains."

Dirt can be excrement. If the co-conspirators wanted to, they could cannibalize the brains of their enemies and turn them into excrement.

Catiline continued:

"Is there a beauty here in Rome you love? An enemy you would kill? What head's not at your mercy? Whose wife, which boy, whose daughter, of what family or class, that the husband or glad parents shall not bring you and boast of the service?"

The co-conspirators would be so powerful that they could have sex whenever they wanted with other people's wives, daughters, and sons. They could also kill whomever they wanted.

Catiline continued:

"Only spare yourselves, and you have all the earth beside, a field to exercise your longings in.

"I see you aroused and confident and read your forward — ardent — minds eager in your faces."

Catiline then called to the servants, "Bring the wine and blood you have prepared there."

Adult servants and pages arrived, carrying wine mixed with blood, and drinking bowls. Pages are boys who are servants.

"What is this?" Longinus asked.

Catiline said:

"I've killed a slave and have caused his blood to be mixed with wine. Fill every man his drinking bowl. There cannot be a fitter drink to make this oath in.

"Here I begin the sacrament to all. Oh, for a clap of thunder now, so loud as to be heard throughout the universe, to tell the world the fact and to applaud it.

"Be firm, my hand, shed not a drop, but pour fierceness into me with it, and cruel thirst of more and more, until Rome be left as bloodless as ever her fears made her, or the sword, and when I cease to wish this to you, stepdame — Rome — or stop working to effect it, with my powers fainting, so may my blood be drawn, and so drunk up as is this slave's."

"And so be my blood," Longinus said.

"And mine," Lentulus said.

"And mine," Autronius said.

"And mine," Vargunteius said.

They drank.

"Fill my bowl yet fuller — to overflooding," Cethegus said. "Here I drink this blood as I would drink Cato's, or the new fellow Cicero's, with that vow which Catiline has given."

Cicero was a *novus homo*, a new man, the first in his family to become so prominent — a Senator and a Consul — in Rome.

"So do I," Curius said.

"And I," Laeca said.

"And I," Bestia said.

"And I," Fulvius said.

"And all of us," Gabinius said.

They drank again.

"Why, now's the business safe and each man strengthened and made sure of," Catiline said.

Seeing one of his serving-boys respond with aversion to Bestia's sexual advances to him, Catiline said to the page, "Sirrah, what ails you?"

"Nothing," the page answered.

"He is somewhat modest," Bestia said.

The page knelt before Catiline.

Catiline said to the page, "Slave, I will strike your soul out with my foot, if I find you again with such a face of aversion, you whelp —"

"Nay, Lucius," Bestia said.

Lucius Sergius Catiline said to the page, "Are you acting coyly, when I command you to be free and open and affable to all?"

In order to achieve his ends, Catiline was willing to allow his co-conspirators to commit sodomy with his boy-servants.

Bestia whispered to Catiline, "You'll be observed."

Catiline said to the page, "Arise, and if you show any least aversion in your look to a man who attempts to jest or to tilt with — board — you next, then your throat opens with a slit."

Catiline could and would do this: The page was a slave, and Catiline was ambitious.

Catiline then said to the co-conspirators:

"Noble confederates and allies, thus far is perfect. Only I will expect your votes at the assembly for the choosing of Consuls, and all the votes you can get from friends to elect me as Consul. Then let me work out your fortunes and my own fortune.

"In the meanwhile, let all of us rest sealed up and silent, as when hard frosts have bound up brooks and rivers, forced wild beasts into their caves, and birds into the woods, countrymen into their houses, and the country sleeps, so that, when the sudden thaw comes, we may break upon them like a deluge, bearing down half of Rome before us, and invade the rest with cries and noise able to wake the urns of those who are dead, and make their ashes fear.

"The horrors that strike the world should come loud and unlooked for. Until they strike, be dumb and do not speak about this plot."

"Oracular Sergius!" Cethegus said.

"God-like Catiline!" Lentulus said.

They all exited.

CHORUS (End of Chapter 1)

The Chorus appeared and spoke in rhyming couplets, lamenting that Rome, although so great and powerful, should be threatened as a result of an excess of plenty, wealth, and ease:

Can nothing great and at the height
Remain so long, but its own weight
Will ruin it? Or is't [is it] blind Chance
That still [always] desires new states t'advance [to advance new states]
And quit the old? Else, why must Rome
Be by itself now overcome?
Has she not foes enough of those
Whom she hath [has] made such, and enclose
Her round about [surround her]? Or are they none,
Except [Unless] she first become her own [her own foe]?
O wretchedness of greatest states,
To be obnoxious to [subjected to] these fates,
That cannot keep what they do gain,
And what they raise so ill sustain.
Rome now is mistress of the whole
World, sea, and land, to either pole;
And even that fortune will destroy
The power that made it. She doth joy [does enjoy]
So much in plenty, wealth, and ease,
As [That] now th' [the] excess is her disease.

The Chorus then described some of Rome's luxuries, including luxuries that made men effeminate:

She builds in gold, and to the stars,
As if she threatened heav'n [heaven] with wars,
And seeks for hell in quarries deep,
Giving the fiends that there do keep [dwell],
A hope of day. Her women wear
The spoils of nations, in an ear,
Changed [Exchanged] for the treasure of a shell [a pearl],

And in their loose attires [loosely fitting dresses] do swell [puff up]
More light [Lighter] than sails, when all winds play.
*Yet are the men more loose [effeminate, loosely dressed, wanton, unchaste]
than they,*
More kempt [combed], and bathed, and rubbed, and trimmed,
More sleeked [smoothed], more soft, and slacker limbed,
As [As a] prostitute: so much that kind [nature]
May seek itself there and not find.
They eat on beds of silk and gold,
At ivory tables or wood sold
*Dearer than it [North African cedar was very expensive], and, leaving plate
[setting aside gold and silver bowls],*
Do drink in stone of higher rate [from bowls set with expensive jewels].
They hunt all grounds and draw [fish in] all seas,
Fowl [Hunt fowl in] every brook and bush, to please
Their wanton tastes, and in request
Have [seek after] new and rare things, not the best.

The Chorus next credited the virtue of Rome's past to "simple poverty."
Now that Rome was rich, it had lost much virtue:

Hence comes that wild and vast expense
That hath [has] enforced [compelled] Rome's virtue thence [to leave],
Which simple poverty first made.
And now ambition doth [does] invade
Her state with eating avarice [avarice that devours everything],
Riot [Debauchery], and every other vice.
Decrees are bought, and laws are sold,
Honors, and offices for gold;
The people's voices [votes], and the free
Tongues in the Senate, bribed be [are bribed].
Such ruin of her manners [conduct and customs] Rome
Doth [Does] suffer now as [now that] she's become,
Without [Unless] the gods it soon gainsay [soon prevent it],
Both her own spoiler [despoiler] and own prey.

The Chorus next blamed the luxuries of Asia, which had been imported to
Rome, for corrupting Rome, thus giving Asia revenge for being conquered:

So, Asia, are you cru'lly [cruelly] even
With us for all the blows you given [that you were given],
When we, whose virtue conquered you,
Thus by your vices ruined be [are ruined].

Catiline and his co-conspirators looked at the excesses of the powerful people of Rome and envied them.

The Chorus looked at the same excesses of the powerful people of Rome and deplored them.

CHAPTER 2

— 2.1 —

Fulvia, Galla, and a servant spoke together in a room in Fulvia's house. Galla was a waiting-woman who served Fulvia, who was a woman of rank and who had many affairs.

Fulvia complained, "Those rooms stink extremely."

She then said, "Bring my mirror and table here, Galla."

"Madam," Galla said.

She went into another room — Fulvia's bedchamber — and brought out a mirror and a table.

"Look within, in my blue cabinet, for the pearl sent to me most recently, and bring it to me," Fulvia ordered.

"The pearl from Clodius?" Galla asked.

"From Caius Caesar," Fulvia said. "You're in favor of Clodius still. Or Curius."

Galla exited.

Fulvia said to the servant, "Sirrah, if Quintus Curius comes here, I am not in a fit mood to see him; I keep to my chamber. Give warning so, outside."

"Sirrah" was a title given to a person of lower social class than the speaker.

The servant exited, and Galla returned with the pearl.

"Is this it, madam?" Galla asked.

"Yes, help to hang it in my ear," Fulvia said.

Pearl earrings were one of the luxuries that the Chorus had criticized.

"Believe me," Galla said. "It is a rich one, madam."

"I hope so," Fulvia said. "It would not be worn there otherwise. Finish what you are doing and bind my hair up."

"In the same style as it was yesterday?" Galla asked.

"No, nor the other day," Fulvia said. "When have you ever known me to appear two days in a row with the same hair-dressing?"

"Will you have your hair in the globe or spire?" Galla asked.

The globe and the spire were two different styles of hair dressing.

"Whichever you wish," Fulvia said. "Any style, however you will do it, good impertinence. Your company, if I slept not very well during nights, would make me an errant fool on account of your questions."

Galla began, "Alas, madam —"

Fulvia interrupted, "Nay, gentle half of the dialogue, cease talking."

So far, she had called Galla by the terms "good impertinence" and "gentle half of the dialogue."

"I do it, indeed, just for your exercise," Galla said, "as your physician tells me."

"What?" Fulvia said. "Does he tell you to anger me for exercise?"

"Not to anger you, but to stir your blood a little," Galla said. "There's a difference between lukewarm and boiling, madam."

"By Jove!" Fulvia said. "She means to cook me, I think! Please, stop."

"I mean to dress you, madam," Galla said.

"To dress" means 1) to fix someone's hair, and 2) to prepare food for cooking.

Galla proceeded to do Fulvia's hair.

"Oh, my Juno, be a friend to me!" Fulvia said.

Juno was a goddess who watched over the women of Rome.

Fulvia continued, "Attempting to be a wit, too? Why, Galla, where have you been?"

Fulvia was pretending that Galla had deliberately made a pun on the phrase "to dress."

"What, madam?" Galla asked.

"What have you done with your poor innocent self?" Fulvia asked.

"What do you mean, sweet madam?" Galla asked.

Fulvia answered, "Thus to come forth, so suddenly, a wit-worm?"

A wit-worm is a beginning wit, one who has just emerged like a caterpillar newly emerged from an egg.

"It pleases you to flout — mock — one," Galla said.

She then attempted to change the subject: "I did dream of lady Sempronia —"

"Oh, the wonder is out," Fulvia said. "Did that infect you? Well, and how?"

Dreaming of lady Sempronia must have caused Galla to attempt to be witty. So said Fulvia.

Galla said, "I thought she did discourse the best —"

Fulvia interrupted, "— that ever you heard?"

"Yes," Galla said.

"In your sleep?" Fulvia said. "What did she talk about?"

"About the Republic, madam, and the state," Galla said, "and how she was in debt, and where she meant to raise fresh sums of money. Sempronia is a great stateswoman — she has the ability of a statesman."

"You dreamed all this?" Fulvia asked.

"No, but you know she is as able as a statesman, madam," Galla said, "and she is a mistress of both the Latin language and the Greek."

"Yes, but I never dreamt it, Galla, as you have done, and therefore you must pardon me," Fulvia said.

"Indeed, you mock me, madam," Galla said.

"Indeed, no," Fulvia said. "Tell me more about your learnéd lady. Does she have a wit, too?"

"A very masculine — vigorous — one," Galla replied.

"She is a she-critic of literature, Galla?" Fulvia asked. "And can she compose in verse, and make quick jests, modest or otherwise?"

"Yes, madam," Galla said.

"Can she sing, too?" Fulvia asked. "And play on instruments?"

"Of all kinds, they say," Galla answered.

"And does she dance splendidly?" Fulvia asked.

"Excellently," Galla said. "So well that a bald Senator made a jest and said it was better than an honest — chaste — woman needed to dance."

"Tut, she may bear that jest," Fulvia said. "Few wise women's 'honesties' will do their courtship hurt."

In other words, the lack of chastity of wise women will seldom interfere with their being courted, aka desired, by men.

"She's liberal, too, madam," Galla said.

The word "liberal" meant 1) generous, and 2) free.

"What!" Fulvia said. "With her money or her honor, I ask you?"

"With both," Gallia said. "You don't know which she spares least."

She may have been less sparing of her money, or she may have been less sparing of her honor. The implication was that both her money and her honor were in short supply because she had given away both.

"A comely commendation," Fulvia said.

"Indeed, it is a pity that she is getting old," Galla said.

"Why, Galla?" Fulvia asked.

"Because it is a fact that she is," Galla said.

"Oh, is that all?" Fulvia said. "I thought you had a reason for saying that."

"Why, so I have," Galla said. "She has been a fine lady, and she still dresses herself — but not as well as you, madam — like one of the best in Rome, and she uses cosmetics and hides her signs of aging very well."

Fulvia said, "They say it is rather a mask than a face she wears."

"They wrong her, truly, madam," Galla said. "She does sleek her face with crumbs of bread and milk, and she lies at nights in very neat gloves."

The word "sleek" means "make smooth." She used milk and bread to clean her face and make it sleek and smooth. She also wore gloves at night. The gloves were possibly dampened inside with something to keep her hands sleek and smooth. Today, a woman might put lotion on dry hands and wear gloves to bed.

Galla continued, "But she is obliged recently to seek men for sex more than she is sought for sex — the rumor is — and so she spends money for that purpose."

"You know everything," Fulvia said.

Galla had gotten her inside knowledge of Sempronia no doubt by gossiping with Sempronia's women-servants, and no doubt Galla had gossiped about Fulvia to those women-servants.

Fulvia continued, "But, Galla, what do you have to say about Catiline's lady, Orestilla? There is the gallant, fashionable woman!"

She meant, of course, Catiline's second wife, Aurelia Orestilla.

Galla said:

"She does well. She has very good and very rich suits of clothing, but then she cannot put them on. She doesn't know how to wear a garment. She shall wear all her jewels and gold sometimes, so that her own self appears to be the least part of herself.

"No, truly, as I live, madam, you excel them all with your excellent strength of judgment, and you draw, too, the world of Rome to follow you. You attire yourself so diversely, and with the spirit of always attracting the men with the noblest characters!

"They could make love to your dress, although your face were away, they say."

Galla's praise had gotten away from her. In praising Fulvia's sense of fashion, Galla was making it sound as if the men were more interested in Fulvia's dress than in her face.

Fulvia said, "And if my body were away, too, would they have the better match of it? Say they are not so, too, Galla?"

In other words, say that they are not effeminate men, Galla.

A servant entered.

Fulvia asked, "Now, what news troubles your face?"

The servant answered, "If it pleases you, madam, the lady Sempronia has alighted from her carriage at the gate —"

Galla interrupted, "By Castor, my dream, my dream!"

"By Castor!" was a woman's oath in Rome. Both Castor and his twin brother, Pollux, were gods who were associated with miraculous interventions. Here, Galla had dreamed about Sempronia, and now Sempronia appeared.

The servant continued, "— and comes to see you."

The servant exited.

"For Venus' sake, good madam, see her —" Galla said.

"Peace! Be quiet!" Fulvia interrupted. "The fool is wild and out of her wits, I think."

Galla continued, "— and hear her talk, sweet madam, about state matters and the Senate."

The servant allowed Sempronia, who was of a higher social class than Fulvia, to enter.

Sempronia entered the room and asked, "Fulvia, good wench, how are thou?"

The word "wench" meant "young woman" and was not perjorative.

In this society, a person of higher rank would use "thou," "thee," and "thy" when referring to a person of lower rank. (These terms were also sometimes used affectionately and between equals.)

A person of lower rank would use "you" when referring to a person of higher rank.

"I am doing well, Sempronia," Fulvia answered. "Where are you going so early?"

"To see Aurelia Orestilla," Sempronia said. "She sent for me. I came to invite thee to go with me. Will thou go?"

"I cannot now, truly," Fulvia said. "I have some letters to write and send away."

"Alas, I pity thee," Sempronia said. "I am so very weary because I have been writing all this night to all the tribes and centuries to ask for their voices — their votes — to help Catiline in his election."

Rome had 35 tribes; a century was a group of 100 men. Tribes and centuries were both involved in voting.

Sempronia continued, "We shall make him Consul, I hope, among us. Crassus, I, and Caesar will gain the Consulship for him."

"Is he a candidate for that political office?" Fulvia asked.

"He's the chief candidate," Sempronia said.

Fulvia asked, "Who is standing for election for Consul besides him?"

She then ordered Galla, "Give me some wine, and give me powder for my teeth."

"Here's a good pearl, in truth," Sempronia said.

"A pretty one," Fulvia said.

"A very lustrous one," Sempronia said.

She then answered Fulvia's question about the other candidates for the position of Consul: "There are other candidates for the office: Caius Antonius, Publius Galba, Lucius Cassius Longinus, Quintus Cornificius, Caius Licinius, and that talker Cicero."

Cicero was an excellent writer and orator.

Sempronia continued, "But Catiline and Antonius will be chosen. For four of the others, Licinius, Longinus, Galba, and Cornificius, will give way, and they will not choose Cicero."

"No?" Fulvia said. "Why?"

"It will be opposed and thwarted by the nobility," Sempronia answered.

Galla said to herself, "How she does understand public affairs!"

Sempronia continued:

"Nor would it be fit for Cicero to be Consul. He is but a new fellow, not originally here in Rome. Catiline calls him a mere lodger here.

"And the Patricians should do very ill to let the Consulship be so defiled as it would be if Cicero obtained it. He is a perfect upstart who has no pedigree, no house, no coat of arms, no heraldic insignia of a family!"

"He has virtue," Fulvia said.

"Hang virtue!" Sempronia said. "Where there is no blood, no good parentage, virtue is vice, and in him sauciness. Why should he presume to be more learnéd or more eloquent than the nobility? Or boast any quality worthy a nobleman, since he himself is not noble?"

"It was virtue only, at first, that made all men noble," Fulvia said.

Sempronia replied, "I grant you that virtue might have made people noble at first, in Rome's poor age, when her kings and her Consuls held the plow, or gardened well. But now we have no need to dig or lose our sweat for virtue."

In 458 B.C.E., Lucius Quinctius Cincinnatus was plowing when news of his appointment as Dictator of Rome came. As Dictator, he had much power to deal with the crisis then facing Rome. Once the crisis was resolved, he stopped being Dictator and went back to farming.

Sempronia continued, "We have wealth, fortune, and ease, and also we have our ancestors' stock of virtue to draw on and give us a reputation for virtue by association, which will defend us against all newcomers — and can never fail us, while the succession of high members of society to high offices stays."

Nobility has its advantages. Nobles often have ancestors with reputations for virtue. Some of the ancestors' glory rubs off on their descendants. Also, just a few high-born families can often monopolize the highest political offices.

Sempronia continued:

"And must we glorify a mushroom, an upstart, one of yesterday and lacking a long notable family history, a fine speaker, because he has nourished himself on rhetoric by studying in Athens? And must we advance him at our own loss?

"No, Fulvia. There are others who can speak Greek, too, if there were need. Caesar and I have sat upon and judged Cicero; so has Crassus, too, and others. We have all decided on his arrest from rising farther. Yes, we will stop him from rising further."

"Excellent and splendid lady!" Galla said.

"Sempronia, you are beholden to my serving-woman here," Fulvia said. "She admires you.

"Oh, good Galla, how are thou?" Sempronia asked.

"The better for your learned ladyship," Galla replied.

"Is this grey powder a good dentifrice?" Sempronia asked. "Does it clean teeth well?"

"You see I use it," Fulvia answered.

"I have one that is whiter," Sempronia said.

"It may be so," Fulvia said.

"Yet this smells well," Sempronia said.

"And it cleanses very well, madam, and resists the crudities of unhygienic teeth," Galla said.

"Fulvia, I ask thee, who comes to thee now?" Sempronia asked. "Which of our great patricians?"

"Truly, I keep no catalog of them," Fulvia said. "Sometimes I have one, sometimes another, as sexual desire excites their blood."

"Thou have them all," Sempronia said. "In faith, when was Quintus Curius, thy special servant, here?"

"My special servant?" Fulvia asked.

A servant can be a lover.

"Yes, your idolater, I call him," Sempronia said.

"He may be yours," Fulvia said, "if you do like him."

"What!" Sempronia said.

"He does not come here," Fulvia said. "I have forbidden him to come here."

"Venus forbid!" Sempronia said.

"Why?" Fulvia asked.

"He is your so constant lover," Sempronia answered.

"He is so much to the contrary," Fulvia said. "I want to have a change of lovers. So would you, too, I am sure. And now you may have him."

"He's fresh yet, Fulvia," Sempronia said. "Beware how you tempt me."

"Fresh" can mean 1) youthful, and 2) not preserved.

"In faith, for me he is somewhat too fresh, indeed," Fulvia said. "The salt that gave him seasoning and flavor is gone."

"Salt" can mean 1) a seasoning, and 2) sexual desire.

Fulvia continued, "His good gifts are done. He does not yield the crop that he used to yield."

Quintus Curius no longer gave her valuable gifts.

She continued, "And as for the sexual act, I can have secret fellows — male prostitutes — with backs worth ten of him, and these male fellows shall please me, now that the land has fled, a myriad better than him."

A strong back is a sign of a good lover.

Quintus Curius' land had metaphorically fled from him because he had sold his land and spent the money.

Fulvia was a woman who looked at a lover and thought, *How much money does he have left?*

Sempronia said, "And one may command those secret fellows."

"That is true," Flavia said. "These lordings, these petty lords, your noble fauns, they are so imperious, saucy, and rude, and as boisterous and savage as Centaurs, leaping sexually on and mounting a lady at first sight."

Fauns were notably horny minor gods.

Centaurs sometimes became drunk and unable to control their lust. The Centaur Eurytion got drunk at a wedding while visiting the Lapiths and tried to rape the bride but was stopped and punished.

Sempronia said, "And they must be borne both with and out, they think. They think they must be both put up with and humored."

One now obsolete meaning of "to bear out" is "to praise publicly" and "to claim that one has accomplished something."

The lovers expected themselves and their love-making to be praised.

Fulvia said, "Tut, I'll pay attention to none of them all, nor humor them a jot longer than they come laden in the hand and say, 'Here's the one for the other.'"

In other words: Here's the money for the sex. The men, however, would probably not say this so crudely but would use less business-like language.

"Does Caesar give well?" Sempronia asked.

"They who come here shall all give and pay well, if they will have it — sex," Fulvia said. "And they will need jewels, pearl, gold and silver vessels and utensils, or round sums — plenty of money — to buy these sexual favors. I am not taken with a male swan, or a high-mounting bull, as foolish Leda and Europa were, but with the bright gold, as Danaë was."

Jupiter, king of the gods, disguised himself as a male swan so he could sleep with Leda, and he disguised himself as a bull so he could carry Europa on his back from Crete to Europe and sleep with her there. To seduce Danaë, Jupiter appeared before her as a rain of bright gold.

Fulvia continued, "For such a price, I would endure a rough, harsh Jupiter, or ten such thundering and vehement amorous gamesters, and refrain from laughing at them until they are gone, with my much tolerating them."

For bright gold, Fulvia would tolerate rough sex or a gangbang. She also would not laugh in their faces at them for parting with valuables in return for a little sexual excitement — she would laugh after they left.

Sempronia said, "Thou are a most happy wench, who thus can make use of thy youth and freshness in their season and have it to make use of."

Fulvia said to herself, "Which is the happiness."

Sempronia said, "I am now glad to give money to them and to keep music and a continual table to invite them to."

Fulvia said to herself, "Yes, and they study your kitchen more than you."

Sempronia continued, "I metaphorically eat myself and literally ruin myself with borrowing money at usurious interest rates, and I ruin my lord and husband, too, and all my domestic servants and friends besides, in order to procure money for the needful and necessary expenses I must be at to have young lovers; and yet, I scarcely can get young lovers even so."

Fulvia said, "Why, that's because you fancy young faces only, and smooth chins, Sempronia. If you'd love beards and bristles, one with another, as others do, or wrinkles —"

She was interrupted by knocking at the door.

"Who's that?" she said. "Go and find out, Galla."

Galla investigated and said, "It is the party, madam."

"What party?" Fulvia asked. "Has he no name?"

"It is Quintus Curius," Galla said.

"Didn't I tell my servants to say that I kept to my chamber?" Fulvia said.

"Why, so they do," Galla said.

Quintus Curius was insisting on seeing Fulvia.

"I'll leave you, Fulvia," Sempronia said.

"Nay, good Sempronia, stay," Fulvia said.

"In faith, I will not," Sempronia replied.

"By Juno, I don't want to see him," Fulvia said.

"I'll not hinder you," Sempronia said.

"You know he will not be kept out, madam," Galla said.

"No, he shall not be kept out, careful Galla, by my intervention," Sempronia said.

She wanted Curius and Fulvia to meet. It amused her.

Fulvia said, "As I do live, Sempronia —"

Sempronia interrupted, "— what is the need of this?

Fulvia ordered Galla, "Go, say I am asleep and ill at ease."

Sempronia said:

"By Castor, no. I'll tell him that you are awake and you are very well.

"Stay here, Galla.

"Farewell, Fulvia. I know my manners. Why do you labor like this, acting against your real wishes?"

She called, "Quintus Curius, she is, indeed, here, and in good disposition."

She meant that Fulvia was able to see Curius and she was in a good mood.

Sempronia then exited.

"Spite with your courtesy!" Fulvia said. "How I shall be tortured!"

Curius entered the room.

He said, "Where are you, pretty one, who conceal yourself and keep your beauty within locks and bars here, like a fool's treasure?"

"True, she was a fool, when first she showed her treasure to a thief," Fulvia said.

"What, pretty sullenness!" Curius said. "So harsh, and short?"

"The Fool's artillery, sir," Fulvia replied.

In other words, words are the Fool's weapons.

In Ben Jonson's day, Fools, aka jesters, were highly regarded.

"Then take my gown off, for the encounter," Curius said.

He began to take his gown — a man's outer garment — off.

An encounter can be 1) an amorous encounter, or 2) a military encounter.

"Stop, sir," Fulvia said. "I am not in the mood."

"I'll put you in the mood," Curius said.

"Best put yourself in your case again —" Fulvia said

By "case," she meant his gown or cover; however, the word "case" also meant vagina, so her sentence had the unintentional meaning of telling him to have sex with her.

She continued, "— and keep your furious — extravagant and foolish — appetite warm, in preparation for when you have place for it."

"What!" Curius said. "Do you pretend to be shy?"

"No, sir. I am not proud," Fulvia said.

This kind of pride is "sexually aroused." It is a now-obsolete meaning of the word "proud."

"I wish you were proud," Curius said. "You think this state becomes you? By Hercules, it does not."

He showed her the mirror that Galla had earlier brought and said, "Look in your mirror now, and see how scurvily that countenance shows. You would be loath to own it."

"I shall not change it," Fulvia said.

"Indeed, but you must, and relax this bended brow and stop frowning, and you must shoot from your eyes less scorn at me," Curius said. "There is a Fortune coming towards you, dainty, that will take you thus" — he attempted to embrace her — "and set you aloft, to tread upon the head of Lady Fortune's own statue here in Rome."

He was predicting great things for her. She would be so fortunate that she could stand on Lady Fortune's head.

"I wonder who let this promiser in!" Fulvia said.

She asked Galla, "Did you, good diligence? Give him his bribe again."

Lovers would often bribe household servants to gain access to the beloved — or to the sexual object.

Fulvia continued, "Or if you had none, I ask you to demand from him why he is so bold to press thus to my chamber, despite being forbidden both by myself and my servants?"

"What!" Curius said. "This is handsome! And somewhat a new strain — tone — of expression!"

When he gave her expensive gifts, she talked to him with a much different tone of voice.

"My tone of voice is not strained, sir," Fulvia said. "It is not forced, and it is not artificial. It is very natural."

"I have known it otherwise between the parties, though," Curius said.

And between the sheets.

"For your knowledge of what has happened before, thank that which made it," Fulvia said. "It will not be so hereafter, I assure you."

What happened before? Sex.

What made it happen? Expensive gifts.

"No, my mistress?" Curius said.

"No, though you bring the same materials — the same gifts," Fulvia said.

She knew he had no gifts to give her.

"Listen to me," Curius said. "You over-react now when you should show restraint. Recall a little and remember yourself again and think. If you are doing this to trick me or find at what forced distance you can hold your servant — your lover — so that it is an artificial trick, to greater inflame and fire me with desire, fearing my love may need it — as heretofore you have done — why, proceed."

Curius thought that Fulvia might be withholding sex from him in order to inflame his lust all the more.

"As I have done heretofore?" Fulvia asked.

Curius answered, "Yes, when you'd feign your husband's jealousy, when your servants were keeping guard and watching you, and when you'd speak softly and run often to the door or to the window and form strange fears that were not necessary — doing all these things as if the pleasure were less acceptable when it was secure and free from fear of discovery."

The possibility of being discovered in the act can thrill some people.

"You are an impudent fellow," Fulvia said.

"And, when you might better have done it at the gate," Curius said, "but instead you took me in at the casement."

They could very well have had sex outside, but Fulvia would let him in through a window.

According to Curius, Fulvia's husband did not mind Fulvia's affairs, and so they could very well have sex in the garden, but Fulvia preferred pretending that they had to be careful when having sex so that her husband would not find out.

"I take you in?" Fulvia said.

"Yes, you, my lady," Curius said. "And then, when I was in bed with you, you would have your well-taught waiting-woman and look-out here" — he pointed to Galla — "come running and cry, 'Her lord!' and hide me without cause, crushed in a chest, or thrust up in a chimney. This happened even when he, her husband, that tame crow, was not even present and was instead napping at his farm, or, if he had been here and present, he would have kept both eyes and beak sealed up for six sesterces."

A sesterce is a coin of little worth.

Fulvia said, "You have a slanderous, beastly, unwashed tongue in your rude mouth, and your tongue is tasting of yourself, you unmannered lord."

"What is this now!" Curius said.

"It is your title, sir," Fulvia said, "who, since you have lost your own good name, and know not what to lose more, don't care whose honor you wound or whose reputation you poison with it."

Curius had been thrown out of the Senate a few years earlier because of immoral conduct.

Fulvia continued, "You should go and vent yourself in the region where you live: among the suburb-brothels, bawds, and pimps, to which place your broken fortunes have designated and consigned you."

To. "vent himself" meant to "discharge himself." He could be discharging semen there.

"Nay, then I must stop your fury, I see, and pluck the tragic mask off," Curius said.

In ancient drama, actors wore masks. Curius thought that Fulvia was putting on an act.

He now called Fulvia lady Cyprus, a reference to Venus, one of whose major cult centers was located on the island of Cyprus: "Come, lady Cyprus, know your own virtues, quickly."

According to Curius, Fulvia's virtues lay in having sex, not in being a drama queen.

Curius continued, "I'll not be put to the wooing of you thus, afresh at every turn, for all the Venus in you. Yield and be pliant, or by Pollux —"

He drew his dagger and attempted to force her to have sex, but she drew a knife.

Seeing her knife, he said, "What is this now? Will Lais turn into a Lucrece?"

Lais of Corinth and Lais of Hyccara were two famous courtesans.

Lucrece was a Roman woman who was raped by Sextus Tarquinian and then committed suicide. Sextus Tarquinian was the son of the King of Rome,

Lucius Tarquinius Superbus. Because of the rape and subsequent suicide, the Romans drove the king and his family out of Rome and formed a republic.

Fulvia differed from Lucrece in that Lucrece stabbed herself with her knife, and Fulvia was prepared to stab Curius.

"No," Fulvia said, "but by Castor, hold off your rapist's hands! I will pierce your heart if you don't. I'll not be put to kill myself, as she did, for you, sweet Tarquin."

Curius began to retreat.

Fulvia said, "What! Do you fall off? Nay, it becomes you graciously. Put not up."

To "fall off" meant 1) to withdraw, and 2) to lose one's erection.

"Put not up" meant 1) Don't put your sword or dagger in its sheath, and 2) Don't put your "sword" or "dagger" in my vagina. The Latin word *vagina* means "sheath."

The word "weapon" can mean "penis."

She continued, "You'll sooner draw your weapon on me, I think, than on the Senate, who have cast you forth disgracefully, to be the common tale of the whole city, you base, infamous man!"

A common tale is the subject of much gossip.

A common tail can be a publicly available penis.

Curius had been thrown out of the Senate because of his immorality.

Fulvia continued, "For, if you were a different man, you would there employ your desperate dagger!"

The "dagger" that he would draw on Fulvia was his penis. But according to Fulvia, if Curius were a different kind of man, the dagger that he would draw on the Senate would be a real dagger.

Putting up his dagger, Curius said, "Fulvia, you know the strengths — the superior powers — you have upon me. Do not use your power too like a tyrant; I can bear almost until you break me."

He could bear her — put up with her — almost until she broke him.

"I do know, sir," Fulvia said. "So does the Senate, too, know you can bear."

Curius had to bear the infamy of being thrown out of the Senate because of his immorality.

"By all the gods, the Senate will smart deeply for your upbraidings," Curius said. "If I were you, I should be very sorry if I — Curius — were to have the means so to be avenged on you — at least the will — as I shall shortly on them. But go on still. Continue. Fare you well, dear lady. You could not still be fair unless you were proud. You will repent these moods, and before long, too. I shall have you come about and change direction again."

Curius hoped to become a rich and powerful man after the revolution against the Senate. If that happened, Fulvia would change her opinion about him.

"Do you think so?" Fulvia asked.

"Yes, and I know so," Curius said.

"By what augury?" Fulvia asked.

"By the fair entrails of the matrons' chests — their treasure-chests — which are gold, pearls, and jewels here in Rome, which Fulvia will then, but too late, say that she might have shared, and, grieving, miss," Curius said.

She would miss out on the wealth that Curius would have after the revolution succeeded.

Fulvia began, "Tut, all your promised mountains and seas, I am so stalely and tediously acquainted with —"

Because Curius could no longer afford to give her valuable gifts, he had begun to promise her great things — figurative mountains and seas.

Curius interrupted, "— but when you see the universal flood run by your coffers; when you see that my lords, the Senators, are sold for slaves, their wives sold for slave-women, their houses and fine gardens given away, and all their goods put under the spear and auctioned in public with loud cries, and you see that you have none of this, but are still Fulvia, or perhaps less, while you are thinking of it. You will advise then, Miss Coyness, with your cushion — you will talk to your pillow — and look on your fingers and say how you were wished for, desired, and invited — and so he left you."

She would look at her fingers and imagine the valuable rings that could be adorning them if she had continued to be Curius' mistress.

Curius exited.

"Call him back again, Galla," Fulvia said.

Galla exited.

Fulvia said to herself, "This is not usual; something hangs on this that I must win out of him. Yes, something is going on, and I need to get him to tell me what it is."

Curius returned.

"How are you now?" Curius asked. "Do you melt?"

"Come, will you laugh now at my easiness?" Fulvia said. "But it is no miracle: Doves, they say, will bill — kiss — after their pecking and their murmuring."

"Yes, and then it is kindly and natural between them," Curius said. "I would have my love angry sometimes, to make the rest of her behavior sweeter by contrast."

"You do see, then, that I study how I may please you," Fulvia said. "But do you think, Curius, that it is covetousness that has made me change my mind? If you love me, change that unkind thought."

"By my loved soul, I love you like I love my soul," Curius said, "and it is my study, more than my own revenge, to make you happy."

The revenge was against the Senate for exposing him.

"And it is that just revenge that makes me happy to hear you strive after it — and which, indeed, has won me to you, more than all the hope of what else can be promised," Fulvia said. "I love valor better than any lady loves her face or clothing — than I myself do. Let me become rooted always where I do embrace. But what good means have you to effect it? Shall I know your project?"

"You shall, if you'll be gracious and give me your favors," Curius said.

"I will be as gracious as I can be," Fulvia said.

"And will you kiss me then?" Curius asked.

"As closely as the shells of cockles — mollusks — meet," Fulvia said.

"And print them deep?" Curius asked.

Would she kiss him hard?

"Quite through our subtle, delicate lips," Fulvia answered.

"And often?" Curius asked.

"I will sow kisses, faster than you can reap them," Fulvia said. "What is your plot?"

"Why, now my Fulvia looks like her bright name, and she is herself!" Curius said.

The Latin word *fulvus* (feminine form *fulva*) means gold-colored.

"Nay, answer me: What is your plot?" Fulvia said. "I request that you tell me, Quintus."

"Aye, these sounds become a mistress," Quintus Curius said.

She kissed and flattered him as he spoke.

Curius continued, "Here is harmony! When you are harsh, I see, the way to bend you is not with violence, but instead with service and compliance. Cruel, a lady is a fire; gentle, a lady is a light."

"Won't you tell me what I ask you?" Fulvia asked.

"All that I can think, sweet love, or that my breast holds, I'll pour into you," Curius said.

"What is your design — plan — then?" Fulvia asked.

"I'll tell you," Curius said. "Catiline shall now be Consul. But you will hear more, shortly."

Fulvia said, "Nay, dear love —"

"I'll tell you while I am in your arms," Curius said. "Let us go into your bedchamber. Rome will be sacked; her wealth will be our prize. By public ruin, private spirits — men of courage — must rise."

"Spirit" can metaphorically mean semen, and "must rise" can refer to an erection. "Public ruin" can mean the loss of a woman's reputation.

Curius and Fulvia exited to go to bed together.

CHORUS (End of Chapter 2)

Catiline and his co-conspirators wanted him to be elected Consul so that they could gain power and loot the city.

The Chorus, however, appeared now and spoke about the need for good government. He also mentioned what the qualities of a good Consul would be.

The Chorus began by praying to Mars, god of war, and to Jupiter, king of the gods:

Great father Mars, and greater Jove,

By whose high auspices [divine protection] Rome hath [has] stood

So long, and first was built in blood

Of your great nephew [nephew = descendant; Remus was Mars' son and Jupiter's grandson], that [who] then strove

Not with his brother but your rites:

Romulus and Remus, twin brothers, took auspices to determine after whom the city they were building should be named. The auspices said that the city should be named Rome after Romulus. Remus disagreed with the auspices, the two brothers fought, and Romulus killed Remus.

The Chorus next spoke about the election then occurring and prayed that the right kind of Romans — ones who cared about Rome — be elected Consuls:

Be present to her now, as then,

And let not proud and factious men

Against your wills oppose their mights.

Our Consuls now are to be made:

Oh, put it in the public voice

To make a free and worthy choice,

Excluding such [e.g. Catiline] as would invade [attack]

The commonwealth. Let whom we name

Have wisdom, foresight, fortitude,

Be more with faith than face [pretense, effrontery] endued [endowed],

And study conscience above fame.

The Chorus named other good qualities of men who should be elected Consul. Let these men be:

Such as not seek to get the start [gain the political advantage]
In state by power, parts [possessions, or factions], or bribes,
Ambition's bawds, but move the tribes
By virtue, modesty, desert.
Such as to justice will adhere,
Whatever great one it offend,
And from th' [the] embraced truth not bend
For envy, hatred, gifts, or fear.
That [Who] by their deeds will make it known
Whose dignity they do sustain,
And life, state, glory, all they gain
Count [They account, aka regard as] the Republic's, not their own.

The Chorus mentioned some Roman families who had served Rome well:

Such the old Bruti, Decii were,
The Cipi, Curtii, who did give
Themselves for Rome and would not live
As men good only for a year [the year of their Consulship].
Such were the great Camilli, too,
The Fabii, Scipios, that [who] still [always] thought
No work at price enough [too high a cost] was bought
That for their country they could do.
And to her honor so did knit [grow together]
As all their acts were understood
The sinews of the public good,
And they themselves one soul with it.
These men were truly magistrates;
These [These men] neither practiced force [violence] nor forms [manipulation of the political rules],
Nor did they leave the helm in storms;
And such [men as] they are make happy states.

The Chorus had referred to many famous Roman families in his speech. These are some of the members of those families:

L. Junius Brutus led the Romans when they deposed the last of the Roman kings and started the Roman Republic.

Publius Decius Mus and his son and grandson, each having the same name as his, saved Rome by fighting well and sacrificing themselves in battle.

Genucius Cipus. According to legend, when Cipus was leaving Rome, horns grew on his head. Soothsayers said that this meant that Cipus would become king when he returned to Rome. Rather than become king, Cipus voluntarily exiled himself. Cipus, a legendary figure, was a Praetor. He declined to become king because he did not want to end the Roman Republic, believing that Romans who served a king would be no better than slaves.

Marcus Curtius saved Rome by sacrificing himself. In 362 B.C.E., a chasm opened in the Roman Forum and could not be filled in. Soothsayers said that the only way the chasm could be closed was by the sacrifice of what was most valuable in Rome. Marcus Curtius, a young soldier, said that the most valuable possession of Rome was the courage of its citizens, and he rode his horse directly into the chasm, which closed behind him.

M. Furius Camillus went into voluntary exile after being falsely accused of embezzlement. After the Gauls sacked Rome, the Romans recalled him and he led the Romans to military victory over their enemy.

Quintus Maximus Fabius Rullianus attacked and defeated the Samnites against the orders of his superiors.

Quintus Maximus Fabius Cunctator (the above's great-grandson) minimized the damage that the great Carthaginian general Hannibal did in Italy through a tactic of delaying. He harassed Hannibal's army but did not meet it in open battle. *Cunctator* is Latin for "the Delayer."

Publius Cornelius Scipio Africanus fought bravely in the Second Punic War and defeated Hannibal by taking the war to Carthage and forcing Hannibal to leave Italy and fight the Romans in Africa.

His adoptive grandson, Publius Cornelius Scipio Africanus Aemilianus, conquered and destroyed Carthage in the Third Punic War.

CHAPTER 3

— 3.1 —

The results of the election were in.

Catiline had failed to become Consul; instead, Cicero had just been elected Consul, along with Antonius. Catiline and the co-conspirators were shocked by the results of the election.

Cicero, Cato, Catulus, Antonius, Crassus, Julius Caesar, the Chorus, some citizens, and some Lictors stood together following the election. The Lictors served the Consuls and carried the fasces: symbols of the Consul's power.

Cicero now began his victory speech:

"Great honors are great burdens; and when they are cast with opprobrium and odium on a man, that man bears two loads. His cares must always be double to his joys in any dignity where, if he would err, he finds no pardon and, for doing well, a very small praise, and that wrung out by force.

"I speak this, Romans, knowing what the weight of the high responsibility and position you have trusted to me is.

"Not that thereby I would wish to appear to undervalue the goodness or greatness of your benefit, for I ascribe it to your singular grace and favor and vow to owe it to no other cause or entitlement, except the gods, that I, Cicero, am your Consul.

"I have no funeral-urns containing the ashes of my ancestors, no dusty ancestral monuments, no broken images of ancestors lacking an ear or nose, no forged tables of long descents from ancestors, to boast false honors from or be my sureties to your trust.

"I am only a new man — as I am styled in Rome — whom you have dignified and, more, in whom you've cut a way, and left it open for virtue — excellence — hereafter, to that place which our great men held shut up, with all ramparts, for themselves."

The word "hereafter" showed that Cicero believed that he had set a precedent for more Consuls who were well qualified for high office because of their excellence, although they lacked great ancestors.

Cicero continued:

"Nor have but few of them — those well qualified for high office because of their excellence — in the past been made your Consuls; new men, before me, none.

"At my first candidacy, in my just year, preferred to all competitors, and some the noblest —"

Cicero's just year was the year in which he first became eligible to be a candidate for Consul: the year he turned forty-three years old.

Catiline, whom Cicero had defeated in the election, came from one of Rome's noblest families.

Crassus whispered to Julius Caesar, "Now the vein — the style of rhetoric — swells."

Crassus was also punning on the word "vein." He believed that Cicero was vain.

Caesar said to Crassus, "Up glory!"

Caesar expected Cicero to glory in his victory.

Cicero continued:

"— and to have your loud consents from your own uttered voices, not silent voting tablets in the secret ballot, nor votes from the meaner tribes. Your loud consents have elected me Consul, but first and last, the universal concourse has elected me Consul: All of Rome's social classes supported me and elected me Consul.

"This is my joy, my gladness."

The votes had actually been cast by writing a candidate's name on a tablet in a secret ballot, but Cicero was stressing the vocal acclaim that the people — including high-born people — had made when he was announced as a winner of one of the two Consul positions.

Cicero was also stressing the vocal acclaim of the Senators and the upper class, whose votes counted more than the votes from the meaner tribes. Often the winner of the election was known before the meaner tribes voted.

Of course, not everyone acclaimed Cicero's victory. Catiline and his supporters did not.

Cicero continued:

"But my care, my industry, and my vigilance now must work, so that always your opinions about me will be approved both by yourselves and by those candidates whom you have rejected and over whom you have preferred me.

"Two things I must labor for: That they who lost the election do not upbraid you and that you do not repent your vote.

"For every lapse of mine will now be called your error, if I make such lapses. But my hope is so to bear myself throughout my Consulship that spite shall never wound you, although it may wound me.

"And for myself I have prepared this strength to act so well as Consul that if evil should happen to me, it shall make the gods to blush, and it shall be their crime, not mine, that I am regarded with ill-will."

Caesar said to himself, "Oh, confidence, newer than is the man!"

Cicero continued:

"I know well in what terms I do receive the commonwealth, how vexed, how perplexed, in which there's not that evil or ill fate that good men fear not and wicked men expect not."

He meant that the evil currently in the commonwealth was evil that good men fear and bad men expect.

Cicero continued:

"I know, besides, that some turbulent conspiracies are already on foot, and rumors of more dangers —"

Crassus said quietly, "Or you will make them, if there are none."

Crassus believed that Cicero would make up a conspiracy if there were none so that he could "save" Rome from it. A Consul can't be a hero unless there's something to be heroic about.

Cicero finished his speech:

"Last, I know it was this which made the envy and pride of the great Roman blood abate and give way to my election."

Cato, one of Marcus Tullius Cicero's supporters, said, "Marcus Tullius, that is true: Our need made you our Consul, and your virtue also made you our Consul."

Caesar whispered, "Cato, you will undo and ruin him with your praise."

Cato whispered back, "Caesar will hurt himself with his own envy."

The Chorus said, "The voice of Cato is the voice of Rome."

A Latin proverb stated, "*Vox populi, vox dei.*" It means, "The voice of the people [is] the voice of God."

"The voice of Rome is the consent of heaven!" Cato said. "And that has placed you, Cicero, at the helm, where now you must show yourself a man and master of your art. Each petty hand on deck can steer a becalmed ship —"

Cato meant that any low-ranking sailor could steer a ship in a calm sea.

He continued, "— but he who will steer and carry her to her destinations must know his tides, know his currents, know how to shift his sails, know what she will bear in foul weathers and what she will bear in fair weathers, know where breaches are caused by planks splitting, know her leaks and how to stop them. He must know what sandbanks, what ledges in the sea, what rocks do threaten her. He must know the forces and the natures of all winds, gusts, storms, and tempests. He must know when her keel plows hell and her deck knocks heaven. Knowing how to manage her — the ship — in all these situations befits the name and office of a pilot."

Cicero said:

"All of this care of the state I'll perform, with all the diligence and fortitude I have, not just for my year as Consul but for my life — unless my life be short, and my year as Consul concludes it.

"If my life must be short, let your will be done, beloved gods. This heart shall yet employ a day, an hour that is left me so for Rome's benefit as it shall make a life spring out of my death to shine forever glorious in my deeds.

"The vicious count their years; the virtuous count their acts."

Cicero wanted to count out his life not by the days he had lived, but by the good and notable deeds he had done.

"Most noble Consul!" the Chorus said. "Let us escort him home!"

Cato, Cicero, the Lictors, the citizens, and the Chorus exited.

"A very popular — demagogic — Consul he has grown, I think!" Caesar said.

"How the mob of people clings to him!" Crassus said.

"And Cato leads them!" Caesar said.

Crassus said to Antonius, "You, his colleague, Antonius, are not looked on. No one is paying any attention to you."

Antonius had been elected the other Consul, and he would serve with Cicero.

"No attention is given to me, nor do I care," Antonius said.

Caesar said, "He — I mean you, Antonius — enjoys rest and ease the while. Let the other Consul's — Cicero's — spirit toil and stay awake for it was created for turmoil."

Catulus said, "Yet, if all the reports are true, Caius Caesar, the time has need of such a watch and spirit."

Caesar said:

"Reports? Do you believe them, Catulus? Why, Cicero makes and breeds them for the people, to endear his service to them. Don't you perceive a trick that is so common? Popular men must create strange monsters and then quell them, to make their arts — professional skills — seem something.

"Would you have such a Herculean actor in the scene, and not his Hydra? They must sweat no less to supply their theatrical properties than to express their parts."

A Hydra was a monster that Hercules killed as one of his famous labors. It had nine heads, one of which was immortal. If a mortal head was cut off, two heads grew in its place. Hercules defeated the Hydra by having a nephew cauterize the places where mortal heads grew so that new heads would not grow in their place and by putting a boulder on the immortal head.

"Treasons and guilty men are made in states too often to dignify the magistrates," Crassus said.

"Those states are wretched that are forced to buy their rulers' reputation with their own infamy," Catulus said.

A bad leader could get a reputation as a hero by creating an enemy and then defeating that enemy. For example, a bad leader could pit white-skinned people versus brown- and black-skinned people and then suppress the people who have brown or black skin.

Crassus and Caesar were saying that Cicero could make himself a hero by pretending that a treasonous plot had been laid; Cicero would be a hero if people believed he stopped that nonexistent plot.

"We therefore should take precautions that ours do not," Crassus said.

"Antonius will make that his concern," Caesar said.

"I shall," Antonius said.

"And watch the watcher," Caesar said.

Walking slowly, Catiline, Longinus, and Lentulus approached the group.

"Here comes Catiline," Catulus said. "How does he take his recent loss in the election?"

"I don't know," Caesar said. "But painfully, to be sure."

"Longinus, too, did stand as a candidate for Consul?" Catulus asked.

"At first," Caesar said. "But he gave way to his friend."

Longinus stepped aside in the election in an attempt to have his voters vote for Catiline instead.

"Who's that coming?" Catulus asked. "Lentulus?"

"Yes," Caesar said. "He is again taken into the Senate."

In 70 B.C.E., the Censors threw Lentulus and Curius out of the Senate because of Lentulus' and Curius' immorality. Now Lentulus was again in the Senate.

"And he was made Praetor," Antonius said.

Praetor was a high office, second only to Consul. Lentulus had been elected one of the new Praetors.

"I know it," Catulus said. "He had my vote, immediately after the Consuls voted."

"True, you were there, Prince of the Senate — the Senior Senator — then," Caesar said.

Catulus was *Princeps Senatus*, a position that allowed him to vote after the Consuls. The position had no *imperium*, or power, but having the title was a great honor. In prestige, Catulus ranked just below the Consuls.

Catiline, Longinus, and Lentulus joined the others.

"Hail, noblest Romans!" Catiline said.

He said to Antonius, "The worthiest Consul, I congratulate your honor."

Grammatically, the sentence can be construed as saying that Catiline was the worthiest Consul. "The worthiest Consul" could modify "I." Or it could be in the vocative case and refer to Antonius.

"I could wish that it had been happier by your fellowship, most noble Sergius, had it pleased the people," Antonius said to Catiline.

Antonius and Cicero, but not Sergius Catiline, had been elected Consul.

Lucius Sergius Catiline said, "It did not please the gods, who instruct the people, and their unquestioned pleasures must be served. They know what's fitter for us than ourselves, and it would be impiety to think against them."

"You bear it rightly, Lucius," Catulus said to Catiline, "and it gladdens me to find your thoughts so even and calm."

Catiline replied, "I shall always study to make them such — even and calm — to Rome and heaven."

"Even" can mean 1) peaceful, or 2) equal. Catiline wanted to equal — rival — the gods. He also wanted to be equal — even — to the gods.

He also wanted to make his thoughts even in the sense of getting even with — getting revenge on — Rome and the gods.

Catiline whispered to Julius Caesar, "I would withdraw with you and speak to you a little, Julius."

Caesar whispered back, "I'll come to your home."

He added, "Crassus would not have you speak to him in front of Quintus Catulus."

Catiline whispered to Caesar, "I understand."

Quintus Catulus had quarreled with Crassus. The two men has held the position of Censor together, but Catulus had resigned because he could not get along with Crassus.

Catiline then said to everyone present, "No, when the gods shall judge honors are suitable for me, I shall have them bountifully and with a full hand, I know it. In the meantime, men who obey are no less part of the commonwealth than those who command."

"Oh, let me kiss your forehead, Lucius," Catulus said. "How you are wronged!"

"By whom?" Lucius Sergius Catiline asked.

"By the public report, which gives out that you take offense at your repulse, and brook — endure — it deadly."

The repulse was not being elected Consul.

Catiline said, "Sir, she — *fama*, public report — brooks not me. Instead, believe me, and believe yourself now that you see me. It is a kind of slander to trust rumor."

"I know it," Catulus said. "And I could be angry with it."

"So may not I," Catiline said. "Where it concerns himself, who's angry at a slander makes it true."

Being angry at a slander about oneself can make other people believe that the slander is true.

"Most noble Sergius!" Catulus said. "This equanimity of yours melts me."

Crassus said to Quintus Catulus, "Will you render due respect to the Consul, Quintus?"

He was referring to Antonius, who had been elected Consul along with Cicero.

"The due respect that Cato and the rout have done to the other Consul: Cicero?" Caesar asked.

Catulus said, "I wait until he will go."

He then said to Catiline, "Be always yourself. He who has virtue lacks no personal standing."

Catulus, Antonius, Caesar, Crassus, and the Lictors exited.

Catiline said to himself, "Did I appear to be as tame as this man thinks me? Did I look so poor, so dead? Did I look so like that nothing that he calls virtuous? Oh, my breast, break quickly, and show my friends my inward thoughts, lest they think that I have betrayed them."

"Where's Gabinius?" Longinus asked.

"Gone," Lentulus answered.

"And Vargunteius?" Longinus asked.

"Slipped away, all shrunk now that Catiline has missed the Consulship," Lentulus answered.

Catiline said to himself, "I am the scorn of bondmen — slaves — who are next to beasts. What can I worse declare myself that's fitter? What worse thing can I say about myself? I am the owl of Rome whom boys and girls will mock and hoot at! Or I could say that, if I were set up in the place of that wooden god — Priapus — that keeps our gardens as a scarecrow, I could not frighten the crows or the least bird enough to keep them from excreting on my head."

Longinus and Lentulus continued to speak privately to each other, not listening to Catiline.

"It is strange that Catiline could miss being voted Consul," Longinus said.

"Isn't it stranger that the upstart Cicero should carry the votes so, by all consents, from men who are so much his masters?" Lentulus said.

"That's true," Longinus said.

Catiline said to himself, "To what a shadow am I melted!"

"Antonius won it by only a few votes," Longinus said.

Catiline said to himself, "I have been struck through, as if I were air, and feel it not. My wounds close faster than they're made."

"The whole design — the whole enterprise — has been lost by Catiline's loss in the election," Lentulus said. "All hands quit it upon his failure."

Catiline said to himself, "I grow mad at my patience. It is a visor — mask or helmet — that has poisoned me. I wish that it had burned me up and I died inward, with my heart turned to ashes."

Cethegus entered the scene and walked over to Catiline to join him privately.

"Here's Cethegus yet," Longinus said. He began to pay attention to Catiline.

Catiline said, too loudly, "Repulse upon repulse! An inmate — a new lodger in Rome — elected Consul! I wish that I could reach the axle where the pins are that bolt this frame, so that I might pull them out and pluck all into chaos, with myself!"

The word "axle" also means axis. This society believed that the Earth had an axis passing through it. Catiline wanted to remove the pins holding the axis steady and let the Earth plunge into chaos.

"What! Are we wishing now?" Cethegus said, hearing Catiline's words.

"Yes, my Cethegus," Catiline said. "Who would not fall with all the world about him?"

If Catiline was going to fall, he wanted to take the entire world with him.

"Not I," Cethegus said. "I would stand on the world when it falls and force new nature out, to make another. These wishings are those of a woman, not of a Roman. Let us seek other arms — another form of attack."

The plan to make Catiline a powerful Consul had failed, so now Cethegus wanted to make a new plan.

"What should we do?" Catiline asked.

"We should do, and not wish," Cethegus said. "Something that wishes cannot perform so suddenly that the gods could not anticipate and forestall it and scarcely have time to fear it."

"Oh, noble Caius!" Catiline said.

"It pleases me better that you are not Consul," Cethegus said. "I would not go through open doors; instead, I would break them. I would swim to my ends and accomplish my ends through blood; or I would build a bridge of carcasses and proceed upon the heads of men struck down like piles supporting a bridge, to reach the lives of those who remain and stand. It is then a prey, when danger stops and obstructs and destruction clears the way."

"How you give voice to my feelings, brave soul," Catiline said. "I may not at all times show myself as I really am, for I bend and conceal according to the occasion."

Catiline and Cethegus joined Lentulus and Longinus.

Catiline pointed to Cethegus and said, "Lentulus, this man, if all our fire were out, would fetch down new fire out of the hand of Jove, and rivet Jove to Mount Caucasus, should Jove but frown, and let his own gaunt, ravenous eagle fly at him, to tear his flesh."

Prometheus had stolen fire and taught Humankind to master it. To punish Prometheus, Jupiter, aka Jove, chained him to Mount Caucasus and each day sent an eagle to devour his liver, which grew back each night so the eagle could devour it again the following day.

Cato entered the scene. Cato supported Cicero, not Catiline.

"Peace! Silence! Here comes Cato," Lentulus said.

He did not want Cato to hear Catiline's words.

"Let him come and hear," Catiline said. "I will no more dissemble and pretend to be that which I am not. All of you, leave us. Everyone except Cethegus leave now. I and my beloved Cethegus here alone will undertake this giants' war, and we will carry — win — it."

The giants — the Titans — fought a war against the Olympian gods, but the giants lost the war.

Lentulus and Longinus declined to leave.

"What is the necessity of this?" Lentulus asked.

"Lucius? Sergius, be more wary," Longinus advised Lucius Sergius Catiline.

Ignoring Lentulus and Longinus, Catiline said, "Now, Marcus Cato, our new Consul's spy, what has your sour austerity been sent to explore?"

"Nothing in you, licentious Catiline," Cato said. "Nooses and racks — instruments of torture — cannot wring from you more than your bad deeds have already revealed. It is only judgment that awaits you."

In other words, Catiline's deeds had already proven his guilt. Now all that remained to do was to punish Catiline.

"Whose judgment? Cato's? Shall he judge me?" Catiline asked.

"No, the judgment of the gods, who forever follow — pursue — those they don't go with as benefactors. And the judgment of the Senate, who with fire must purge sick Rome of noisome, unwholesome, harmful citizens, of whom you are one. Be gone, or else I will go. It is poison to breathe the same air with you."

"Strike him!" Caius Cethegus said, drawing his sword.

"Stop, good Caius!" Lentulus said.

"Aren't you afraid, Cato?" Cethegus said.

"Rash Cethegus, no," Cato said. "Something would be wrong with Rome, when Catiline and you threaten, if Cato was afraid."

Cato had spoken of using fire to purge Rome's illness by getting rid of bad citizens.

"The fire you speak of — if any flame of it would approach my fortunes, I'll quench it, not with water but with ruin," Catiline said.

One way to stop a house fire from spreading was to demolish the houses around it.

"You hear this, Romans," Cato said.

He exited.

"Bear it to the Consul," Catiline yelled after Cato.

He meant: Carry my words to Cicero.

"I would have sent away his soul before him," Cethegus said. "I would have killed him instead of letting him leave. You are too sluggish, Lentulus, and remiss. It is for you we labor, and the kingdom promised to you by the Sibyls."

The Sibylline prophecy — as interpreted by augurs whom Catiline had bribed — had stated that Lentulus would become King of Rome.

Catiline said, "A kingdom that Lentulus' Praetorship and some small flattery from the Senate will make him forget."

"You wrong me, Lucius," Lentulus said to Catiline.

"He will not need these spurs to action," Longinus said.

"The action needs them," Catiline said. "These things, when they proceed not forward, they go backward."

"Let us consult then," Lentulus said. "Let's make a plan."

"Let us first take arms," Cethegus said. "They who deny us just things now, will give all that we ask, if once they see our swords."

"Our objectives must be sought with wounds, not words," Catiline said.

Cicero and Fulvia talked together. Fulvia had informed Cicero about Catiline's plot, a plot that Curius had told her about.

Cicero said:

"Is there a heaven and gods, and can it be that they should be so slow to hear and be so slow to see?

"Has Jove no thunder, or has Jove become as torpid and stupefied as you are, nearly wretched Rome, when both your Senate and your gods sleep and neither your nor their own states do keep?

"What will awake you, heaven? What can excite your anger, if this treasonous practice is too trivial?

"Catiline's former plots partake of former times, but this last plot was only Catiline's. Oh, that it would be his last! But he before has safely done so much he'll still dare more.

"Ambition, like a torrent, never looks back and is an increasing swelling of pride and the last affection a high mind can put off, being both a rebel to the soul and reason; and it — ambition — overcomes by force all laws and all conscience, treads upon religion, and offers violence to nature's self.

"But here is that which transcends it! A black purpose to cast into confusion nature, and to ruin that which neither time nor mankind can ever repair and restore.

"Sit down, good lady."

Fulvia sat.

Using the third person, Cicero continued:

"Cicero is lost in this your story: for to think it is true tests my reason. It so far exceeds all the strange and immoderate fictions of the tragedies on stage.

"The commonwealth, still panting underneath the strokes and wounds of a recent civil war, gasping for life, and scarcely restored to hope: To seek to oppress her with new cruelty and utterly extinguish her ancient name with so prodigious and unheard-of fierceness!

"What sink — scum, pit, cesspool — of monsters, wretches of lost minds, mad after change and desperate in their states, wearied and oppressed with their poverty — for all this I acknowledge them to be — dared have thought it?

"Would the barbarous deeds of Marius and Sulla have been believed by our children, had not this greater evil deed arisen forth for them? All that Marius and Sulla did was piety compared to this because they only murdered kinsfolk, brothers, and parents and raped the virgins and perhaps some matrons. They left the city and the temples standing: The gods and the majesty of Rome were safe yet.

"Catiline and his co-conspirators purpose to set on fire Rome, to despoil the temples — beyond the other evils — and lay waste the far-triumphed world — the world over which Rome has triumphed far and wide and in which it is known for its triumphs — for what can be enough for someone to whom Rome is too little room?"

"It is true, my lord," Fulvia said. "I had the same reasoning."

Cicero continued:

"And then to take a horrid sacrament of wine and human blood for the execution of this their dire design, which might be called the height of wickedness, except that for which they did it was higher wickedness still!"

The plotted rebellion was more wicked than the drinking of the mixture of wine and the slave's blood.

Fulvia said, "I assure your lordship that the extreme horror of it almost turned me to injurious air, when first I heard it. I was all vapor when it was told to me, and I longed to vent it anywhere. It was such a secret that I thought it would have burnt me up."

"Good Fulvia, don't fear your act, must less repent of it," Cicero said.

"I do not repent it, my good lord," Fulvia said. "I know to whom I have uttered it."

She had informed Cicero about the plot, and he was in a position of power to stop it.

"You have discharged your duty safely," Cicero said. "Should Rome, for whom you have done the happy service, turn most ungrateful, yet would your virtue be paid in the consciousness of the deed. So much good deeds reward themselves."

In other words: Virtue is its own reward.

"My lord, I didn't do it for any other aim but for itself. I did not do it for any ambition of reward," Fulvia said.

"You have learned the difference between doing office to the public welfare and private friendship, and have shown it, lady," Cicero said. "Be still yourself. I have sent for Quintus Curius, and for your virtuous sake, if I can win him yet to the commonwealth, he shall be safe, too."

"I'll undertake, my lord, that he shall be won to the right side," Fulvia said.

"Please, join with me then, and help to persuade him to do the right thing," Cicero said.

A Lictor entered the room.

"How is it now?" Cicero said. "Has Curius come?"

"He is here, my lord," the Lictor answered.

"Go immediately and tell my colleague Antonius I want to speak with him about some immediate business of the state.

"And, as you go, call on my brother Quintus and tell him, with the Tribunes, to come to me.

"Now tell Curius to enter."

The Lictor exited.

Cicero asked, "Fulvia, you will aid me?"

"It is my duty," Fulvia said.

Curius entered the room.

Cicero said:

"Oh, my noble lord! I have to chide you, truly. Give me your hand. Nay, don't be troubled. It shall be gently, Curius. You look upon this lady? What, do you guess my business yet?

"Come, if you frown, I will thunder. Therefore, put on your better looks and thoughts. There's nothing but fair and good intended to you, and I would make those — your better looks and thoughts — your nature and habit of mind."

Cicero then mentioned Lentulus, who had been restored to the Senate, although Curius had not:

"Would you, of whom the Senate had that hope, as to my knowledge it was in their purpose during the next sitting to restore you, as they have done the stupid and ungrateful Lentulus — excuse me that I name you thus together, for yet you are not such as he is —

"Would you, I say, a person both of blood and honor, coming from a long line of virtuous ancestors, embark yourself for such a hellish action with relative-killers and traitors, men turned Furies out of the waste and ruin of their fortunes — for it is despair that is the mother of madness — despair such as that arising from want and poverty — that which all conspirators, except they, have first — a mere pretext for their evil?"

In other words, Curius' life was good. He came from a long and distinguished line of family members, and he was on the verge of again becoming a Senator. Most conspirators become traitors out of despair, but Curius had nothing to despair about.

Cicero continued:

"Oh, I must blush with you. Come, you shall not labor to extenuate your guilt, but to quit it entirely. Bad men excuse their faults, good men will leave and abandon them. He acts the third crime who defends the first crime."

The three crimes are 1) the evil deed, 2) failure to repent, and 3) self-justification for committing the crime.

Cicero continued:

"Here is a lady — Fulvia — who has got the start in piety of us all, and for whose virtue I could almost turn lover again, except that Terentia — my wife — would be jealous.

"What an honor has Fulvia gained for herself! What voices, titles, and loud applauses will pursue her through every street! What windows will be filled with people who will shoot eyes — gaze — at her! What envy and grief will matrons feel because they are not she! All of this when her act here shall seem worthier a chariot than if Pompey came in triumph through Rome with his captives from Asia chained behind his chariot!

"All this is while she lives. But when she is dead, her very name will be a statue, not wrought for time but rooted in the minds of all posterity, when brass and marble, aye, and the Capitol itself, is dust!"

"Your Honor thinks too highly of me," Fulvia said.

Cicero said:

"No, I cannot think highly enough of you. And I would have Curius emulate you.

"It is no shame to follow the better precedent. She shows you, Curius, what claim your country lays to you, and what duty you owe to it.

"Don't be afraid to break with murderers and traitors for the saving life so near and necessary to you as is your country's life.

"Think only on Rome's right: No child can be too naturally loving to his parent. She is our common mother, and she lays claim to the best part of us; do not stop, but instead give her the best part of you. He who is void of fear may soon be just, and no religion binds men to be traitors."

Fulvia said to Cicero, "My lord, he understands it and will follow your saving counsel and advice. But his shame yet stays him. I know that he is coming around to what you advise."

"Do you know it?" Curius asked Fulvia.

Curius and Fulvia spoke privately apart from Cicero.

"Yes, let me speak with you," Fulvia said.

Curius said, "Oh, you are —"

"What am I?" Fulvia said.

"Don't speak so loudly," Curius said.

Fulvia said, "I am what you should be. Come, do you think I'd take part in any plot where madam Sempronia should take precedence over me, and Fulvia walk in the rear, or be on the side in a place of secondary importance? Do you think that I would be her second in a business, although it might give me everything the sun sees?

"It was a silly fantasy — a foolish dream — of yours. Attach yourself to me and the Consul and be wise. Follow the fortune I have put you into. You may be something this way, and with safety."

Cicero joined them and said, "Nay, I must tolerate no whisperings, lady."

"Sir, you may hear," Fulvia said. "I am telling him how hazardous his course was in the way wherein he was."

Cicero said:

"How hazardous? How certain to all ruin. Did he, or do yet any of the conspirators, imagine that the gods would sleep and pay no attention to such a Stygian — Hellish — practice against the commonwealth that they have founded with so much labor, and with much care have kept now nearly seven hundred years?

According to tradition, Rome was founded in 753 B.C.E.

Cicero continued:

"It is a madness, wherewith heaven blinds them when it would confound them, that they should think it."

A proverb stated, *Quem Deus vult perdere, prius dementat.* Translation: "Whom the god would destroy, he first makes insane."

Cicero continued:

"Come, my Curius, I see your nature's right; you shall no more be mentioned with the conspirators: I will call you mine and trouble this good shame of yours no farther."

Either Curius was ashamed of his actions, or Cicero was pretending that Curius was ashamed of his actions.

Cicero continued:

"Stand firm for your country and become a man who is honored and loved. It would be a noble life to be found dead embracing Rome."

Horace wrote *Dulce et decorum est pro patria mori.* Translation: "It is sweet and fitting to die for one's country."

Cicero continued:

"Do you know what thanks, what titles, what rewards the Senate will certainly heap upon you for your service? Don't allow a desperate action to more engage you than your safety should, and don't allow wicked friendship to force you to do what honesty and virtue cannot persuade you to do."

"He tells you right, sweet friend," Fulvia said. "It is saving counsel that can rescue you."

Curius replied, "Most noble Consul, I am yours and hers — I mean my country's. You have formed me anew, inspiring me with what I should be truly. And I entreat you: Don't let my faith seem cheaper because it springs out of penitence."

"Good Curius, it shall be of greater price rather, and because I'd make it such, hear how I trust you more," Cicero said.

Cicero wanted Curius to be a spy for him:

"Keep still your former face — outward appearance — and mix again with these lost spirits who are the conspirators. Run all their mazes with them, for such are treasons. Find out their windings and subtle turnings, watch their snaky ways through thickets and hedges, into woods of darkness, where they are obliged to creep upon their breasts in paths never trodden by men, but wolves and panthers.

"Learn, beside Catiline, Lentulus, and those whose names I have, what new ones they draw into their plot; who else are likely to join them and be drawn into their plot; who those great ones are they do not name; what ways they mean to take; and whither their hopes point: to war or ruin by some surprise ambush.

"Explore all their intentions and acquaint me with whatever you find that may profit the Republic, either by yourself or by this your virtuous friend, on whom I impose the responsibility of urging you to do the right thing.

"I'll see that Rome shall prove a thankful and a bounteous mother.

"Be as secret as the night."

"And as constant, sir," Curius said.

The night is not constant; it turns to day. Curius is also not constant; he turns from conspirator to anti-conspirator spy.

Cicero said, "I do not doubt it, although lack of time prevents you from making a vow of loyalty to Rome. The dignity of truth is lost with too much protesting."

He called, "Who is there?"

This was a way of calling a servant to escort Curius and Fulvia out of Cicero's house.

A servant entered the room.

Cicero said to Fulvia and Curius, "Leave this way, lest you be seen and met. And when you come, let this be your token to say to this servant."

Cicero gave them the password.

He then said to the servant, "Light their way with torch-fire."

The servant, Curius, and Fulvia exited.

Alone, Cicero said to himself:

"Oh, Rome, in what a sickness have you fallen! How dangerous and deadly, when your head is drowned in sleep, and all your body is feverish!

"Rome, your lethargy is such that no noise, no pulling, no vexation wakes you; or, if by chance you heave your eyelids up, you do forget, sooner than you were told, your own danger. I didn't act reverently when I blamed the gods who wake and watch for you, although you snore to yourself.

"Isn't it strange that you should be so diseased and feel so secure? But, more, isn't it strange that the first symptoms of such a malady should not rise out from any worthy member, but a base and common strumpet, worthless to be named even a hair or other part of you?"

The base and common strumpet was Fulvia, who first informed Cicero about the conspiracy.

Continuing to refer to Rome as "you," Cicero continued:

"Think, think hereafter what your needs were, when you must use such means; and lay it to your breast — remember — how much the gods upbraid your foul neglect of them by making so vile a thing the author of your safety.

"They — the gods — could have worked by nobler ways: They could have struck your foes with forked lightning or blasted thunder; thrown hills upon them in the process; have sent death, like a noxious vapor, to all their families; or caused their consciences to burst them.

"But, when they will show you what you are and make a scornful difference between their power and you, they help you by such aids as geese and harlots."

Enemy soldiers once tried to sneak up the Capitoline Hill, but geese sacred to Juno cackled and alerted the Romans to the approach of the enemy soldiers.

The word "goose" was also slang for "prostitute" in addition to being the name of a kind of fowl.

A Lictor entered the room.

"How is it now?" Cicero asked. "What is the answer? Has he come?"

The Lictor replied, "Your brother will immediately be here, and your colleague Antonius said, coldly, that he would follow me."

The Lictor exited.

Alone again, Cicero said to himself:

"Aye, that troubles me somewhat and is worth my fear. Antonius is a man against whom I must make provisions so that, as he'll do no good, he will also do no harm.

"Antonius, although he is not of the plot, will like it and wish it should proceed; for all change is always welcome to men oppressed by and pressed with their needs.

"I must with offices and patience win him. I must make him by art that which he was not born: a friend to the public and the republic. And so I will bestow on him the province of Macedonia that is by the Senate decreed to me. That benefit will bind him."

Antonius suffered from debt. Since Macedonia was a rich province that would supply him with much money, he need not support a dangerous conspiracy in an attempt to get money to pay his debts.

Consuls normally served as the governor of a province after their Consulship. The provinces were awarded by lot, and Cicero had won the wealthier province, but Cicero would trade Macedonia to Antonius for the less affluent province of Transalpine Gaul. This would make Antonius beholden to Cicero, and Cicero would make him do the right thing.

Cicero continued:

"It is well if some men will do well for reward. So few are virtuous when the reward's away. Nor must I be unmindful of my own private interests, for which I have called my brother and the Tribunes, my kinsfolk, and my clients to be near me."

Tribunes were administrative officers in Rome. Some were judicial Tribunes, and some were military Tribunes.

Cicero was the patron to some people of lower status than himself. They were his clients, and they had obligations to him as he had to them.

His private interests included self-protection. The conspirators wanted him dead.

Cicero continued:

"He who stands up against traitors and their ends shall need a double guard of law and friends, especially in such an envious state that sooner will accuse the magistrate than the delinquent and will rather grieve that the treason is not acted, than believe."

Julius Caesar and Catiline spoke together in the house of co-conspirator Laeca.

Caesar said:

"The night grows later, and you are about to have your meeting. I'll therefore end with a few words.

"Be resolute and put your plan in action. The more that actions of gravity, deep significance, and danger are considered, the less assuredly they are performed. And thence it happens the bravest and most splendid plots that are not executed immediately have been discovered. Say you are constant, or another, a third, or more, there may be yet one wretched spirit with whom the fear of punishment shall work above all the thoughts of honor and revenge.

"You are not now to think what's best to do, as in the beginnings of a plot; instead, you are to think what must be done, now that the plot has thus begun, and you are to let pass no advantage that may secure you.

"Let them call it evil now. When it is past and has prospered, it will be called virtue. Petty crimes are punished, but great crimes are rewarded.

"Nor must you think of peril, since attempts and essays begun with danger always end with glory. And when need spurs action, despair will be called wisdom.

"Less ought the anxiety about men or reputation to frighten you, for they who win seldom receive shame from their victory, however it has been achieved, and they receive vengeance least.

"For who, besieged with wants and needs, would stop at death, or anything beyond it?

"Come, there was never any great thing yet attained but by violence, or fraud. And he who balks, because of the folly of a conscience, to reach it —"

Catiline finished Caesar's sentence: "— is a good religious — superstitious — fool."

Caesar agreed:

"He is a superstitious slave, and he will die a beast, not a man.

"Good night. You know what Crassus thinks, and I, by this: Prepare for yourself wings, as large as sails, to cut through air and leave no impression behind you.

"A serpent, before it comes to be a dragon, eats a bat, and so must you 'eat' a Consul who watches and guards."

A Greek proverb stated, "Unless a serpent eat a serpent, he will not become a dragon." The proverb meant that to advance one must make someone else fail.

Caesar then said to Sergius Catiline, "What you do, do quickly, Sergius."

This is John 21-27:

21 When Jesus had thus said, he was troubled in spirit, and testified, and said, Verily, verily, I say unto you, that one of you shall betray me.

22 Then the disciples looked one on another, doubting of whom he spake.

23 Now there was leaning on Jesus' bosom one of his disciples, whom Jesus loved.

24 Simon Peter therefore beckoned to him, that he should ask who it should be of whom he spake.

25 He then lying on Jesus' breast saith unto him, Lord, who is it?

26 Jesus answered, He it is, to whom I shall give a sop, when I have dipped it. And when he had dipped the sop, he gave it to Judas Iscariot, the son of Simon.

27 And after the sop Satan entered into him. Then said Jesus unto him, That thou doest, do quickly. (King James Version)

Preparing to leave, Caesar said, "You shall not stir for me."

By "shall not stir," he meant that Catiline need not make a fuss.

"Excuse me," Catiline said.

He intended to stir himself to help Caesar get where he was going.

He called to servants outside the room, "Lights there!"

Catiline was calling a servant to bring a torch to light Caesar's way.

"By no means," Caesar said.

This was supposed to be a secret meeting. Having a servant light his way as he left would make him more noticeable.

Catiline called to the servants, "Stay then."

He then said to Caesar, "All good thoughts to Caesar! And the same to Crassus."

"Just bear in mind your friends' counsels and advice," Caesar said.

He exited, alone.

"Or I will lack spirit," Catiline said.

He meant that he would lack courage if he did not bear in mind his friends' counsels and advice.

His wife, Aurelia, entered the room.

"How are you now, Aurelia?" Catiline said. "Have your confederates come? The ladies?"

"Yes," Aurelia said.

"And is Sempronia there?" Catiline asked.

"She is," Aurelia answered.

"That's well," Catiline said. "She has a sulfurous — fiery — spirit and will take light at a spark. Broach the subject to them, gentle love, about drawing as many of their husbands into the plot as they can. If not, to get rid of them: That'll be the easier practice for some wives who have been long tired of them."

One way to get rid of an unwanted husband is to have them die in the rebellion.

Catiline continued, "Solicit their aids for money, and their servants' help in setting fire to the city at the designated time. Promise them states, and empires, and men for lovers, made of better clay than ever the old potter Titan knew."

Prometheus, one of the Titans, made men out of clay and the goddess Athena breathed life into them.

Laeca, whose house they were in, entered the room.

"Who's that?" Catiline said. "Oh, Porcius Laeca! Are they here?"

"They are all here," Porcius Laeca said.

Catiline said to Aurelia, "Love, you have your instructions. I'll trust you with the stuff — the material — you have to work on. You'll give form to it."

Aurelia would work at persuading the women to convince their husbands to support the rebellion.

Catiline then said to Porcius Laeca, "Porcius, fetch the silver eagle I gave into your keeping."

The eagle was depicted on a battle standard, aka battle flag.

Catiline added, "And ask them to enter the room."

Laeca exited.

Cethegus, Curius, Lentulus, Vargunteius, Longinus, Gabinius, Ceparius, Autronius, and Cornelius entered the room.

"Oh, friends, your faces gladden me," Catiline said. "This will be our last meeting, I hope, of consultation."

"So it had better be," Cethegus said.

"Daily we lose the opportunity to act," Curius, who was now acting as a spy for Cicero, said.

"Aye, and our means, whereof one wounds me most — that was the fairest. Piso is dead, in Spain," Catiline said.

Piso had been murdered. One rumor was that Pompey had instigated the murder. Another rumor was that some Spaniards had murdered him because of his cruel rule.

"As we are, here," Cethegus said.

Cethegus was a hothead who wanted violence — now.

"And, as it is thought, by the malice of Pompey's followers," Longinus said.

"He also is coming back now, out of Asia," Lentulus said.

Pompey's army, if it returned, would likely oppose Catiline.

Catiline said:

"Therefore, what we intend we must be swift in. Take your seats and listen.

"I have already sent Septimius into the Picene territories, and Julius to raise an army for us in Apulia. Manlius at Faesulae is by this time ready for war, with the old needy troops who followed Sulla; and they just wait until we will give the blow at home."

Laeca entered with the eagle battle standard.

Catiline said:

"Behold this silver eagle. It was Marius' standard in the Cimbrian war, and it was fatal to and influencing the fate of Rome, and, as our augurs tell me, shall still be so; for which single ominous, portentous cause I have kept it safe and done it sacred rites as if to a godhead, in a chapel built expressly for it. "

Marius won the war against the Cimbrians and so kept Rome safe; the word "fatal" meant "connected with [Rome's] fate." Catiline's rebellion, however, if successful, would be fatal in another sense to the Roman Republic.

Catiline continued:

"Clasp then all your hands as a pledge to follow this battle standard, with vows of death and ruin struck silently and home."

The conspirators made their vows, silently.

Catiline continued:

"So waters speak when they run deepest.

"Now's the time. This year is the twentieth year from the burning of the Capitol, as fatal, too, to Rome, by all predictions. And in which honored Lentulus must rise and become a king, if he pursues it."

"If he does not, he is unworthy of the great destiny," Curius said.

"This destiny is too great for me," Lentulus said, "but what the gods and their great loves decree me, I must not seem inattentive to."

"No, nor must we be envious," Catiline said. "We have enough beside: all Gallia, Belgia, Greece, Spain, and Africa."

These were regions that the conspirators would split up among themselves.

"Aye, and Asia, too," Curius said, "now that Pompey is returning."

"Noblest Romans," Catiline said, "I think our looks are not as quick and high — as fiery and noble — as they used to be."

"No?" Curius said. "Whose is not?"

Catiline said, "We have no anger in our eyes, no storm, no lightning. Our hate is spent and fumed away in vapor, before our hands are at work. I can accuse not any one person, but I can accuse all of slackness."

"Yes, and accuse yourself as such, while you do it," Caius Cethegus said.

"What?" Catiline said. "That is sharply answered, Caius."

"Truly, truly," Cethegus said.

Lentulus said, "Come, let each of us know his part to do, and then let us be accused. Set aside these untimely quarrels."

"I wish there were more Romes than one to destroy and ruin," Curius said.

"More Romes?" Cethegus said. "More worlds."

"Nay, then more gods, and natures, if they took part," Curius said.

Curius was out-doing Cethegus in talking about violence, something that was difficult to do. Curius was even blaspheming.

"When shall the time be, first?" Lentulus said.

"I think the Saturnals," Catiline said.

"It will be too long to wait," Cethegus said. "That's too far off in time."

"They are not far off," Catiline said. "It is not a month."

"A week, a day, an hour is too far off," Cethegus said. "Now would be the fittest time."

"We have not laid — arranged — all things so safe and ready," Catiline said.

Caius Cethegus said, "While we're delaying, we shall all lie and grow to earth. I wish that I would have nothing to do with the plot, if we do not put it in action now. These things, they should be enacted before they are thought."

One way to grow to earth is to die and be buried in a burial plot.

"Nay, now your reason forsakes you, Caius," Catiline said. "Think but what convenience that time will furnish: The city's custom is to be then in mirth and feast."

During the Saturnalia, which occurred in the middle of December, slaves had freedom of speech and they ate a meal at which their masters served them. Schools and law courts were closed. Much merriment occurred, and no one would expect a rebellion.

After taking the Trojan Horse into the city of Troy, the Trojans thought that they had won the war, and so they celebrated with much drinking into the night. Their drunkenness made it easier for the Greek army to defeat them after the Greek soldiers hidden inside the Trojan Horse came out, went to the city gates and opened them, letting in the rest of the Greek army.

Lentulus said, "They will be entirely relaxed in pleasure and security —"

Autronius said, "Each house will be relaxed in freedom —"

Curius said, "Every slave will be a master —"

Longinus said, "And they, too, will be no mean aids —"

Curius interrupted, "— made from their hope of liberty —"

Lentulus interrupted, "— or hate to their lords."

Vargunteius said, "It is certain there cannot be a time found out more apt and natural than the Saturnalia to have our rebellion."

Cethegus did not look happy. He looked angry.

Lentulus said, "Nay, good Cethegus. Why do your passions now disturb our hopes?"

"Why do your hopes delude your certainties?" Cethegus asked.

To Cethegus, if the rebellion started *now*, it was certain to be successful.

Catiline said to Cethegus, "You must let him have his way. Think about the arrangement and method of it."

"Yes," Longinus said.

"I don't like setting Rome on fire," Lentulus said. "It will too much lay waste my city."

"Even if Rome were reduced to embers, there will be wealth enough raked out of them to make spring up a new Rome," Catiline said. "It must be fire, or nothing."

Wealth could be raked out of the ashes, but not the souls of the dead.

"What else should frighten or terrify them?" Longinus asked.

"True," Vargunteius said. "In that confusion must be the chief slaughter."

"Then we shall kill them most splendidly," Curius said.

"And in heaps," Ceparius said.

"We will strew sacrifices," Autronius said.

"We will make the earth an altar," Curius said.

Animals were bloodily sacrificed on altars.

"And we will make Rome the fire," Longinus said.

"It will be a noble night," Laeca said.

"And worth all Sulla's days," Vargunteius said.

"When husbands and wives, grandsires and nephews, servants and their lords, virgins and priests, the infant and the nurse, go all to hell together, in a fleet," Curius said.

Cethegus had spoken earlier about the need for a navy to carry the souls of those who died in the Sulla-Marius civil war to the Land of the Dead. Curius used the same image when he spoke about the need of a fleet to carry to the Land of the Dead the souls of those who would soon be dead because of the rebellion.

Catiline said:

"I would have you, Longinus and Statilius, take the charge of setting Rome on fire, which must be at a sign given with a trumpet, done in twelve chief places of the city at once. The flax and sulfur are already stored at Cethegus' house. So are the weapons.

"Gabinius, you with other force — troops — shall stop the pipes and conduits, and you shall kill those who come for water to put out the fire."

"What shall I do?" Curius asked.

"All will have employment, fear not," Catiline said. "Ply the execution."

The execution could be of the plan or of a person.

"For that, trust me and Cethegus," Curius said.

Catiline said:

"I will be at hand, with the army, to meet those who escape.

"And, Lentulus, you surround Pompey's house, to seize his sons alive, for they are the bargaining chips that we must use to make our peace with him.

"Cut up all the other people, as Tarquin did the poppy heads or as mowers do a field of thistles."

Sextus Tarquinius sent a messenger to ask his father, Tarquinius Superbus (the last king of Rome) how he could conquer the city of Gabii. His father, who was in his garden, used his sword or his walking stick to decapitate the tallest flowers. Sextus Tarquinius understood that to mean that he should kill the most important men in the city.

Catiline continued:

"Or else cut up, as plows do barren lands; and strike together against flints and clods — strike against the ingrateful, ungrateful, unpleasant, and flinty Senate and strike against the clod-like common people — until no rage gone before or coming after in history may be equal in weight to yours, even though Horror herself would leap into the scale.

"Moreover, in your violent acts, let the fall of torrents and the noise of tempests, the boiling of the whirlpool Charybdis that threatened Ulysses, the sea's wildness, the eating force of flames, and wings of winds, all be outwrought by your transcendent furies.

"It would have been done before this, had I been Consul. We would have had no stop, no hindrance."

"Whose side is Antonius on?" Lentulus asked. "Is he loyal to us?"

Catiline said, "The other side has won him: Antonius is lost to us. Cicero was born to be my opposition and my obstacle, and he stands in all our ways."

Cicero had given the governorship of Macedonia to Antonius and so won him over to the side of the protectors of the Roman Republic.

"Remove him first," Curius said, referring to Cicero. "Kill him first."

"May that yet be done sooner?" Cethegus said.

By "sooner," he meant before the day that Rome would be set on fire.

"I wish it were done," Catiline said.

"I'll do it," Cornelius and Vargunteius volunteered.

They were willing to murder Cicero.

"It is my province," Cethegus said. "Let no one usurp it!"

"What are your means?" Lentulus asked. "How will you do it?"

"Don't ask," Cethegus said. "He shall die. 'Shall' was too slowly said. He's dying. That is yet too slow. He's dead."

Catiline said to Cethegus, "Brave, peerless Roman, whose soul might be the world's soul — *anima mundi* — if that were dying, don't refuse yet the aids of these your friends."

"Here's Vargunteius, who has good relations with Cicero," Lentulus said.

Catiline said, "And under the pretext of clientele — attendance on a patron — and visitation with the morning 'hail,' he will be admitted."

Clients traditionally paid a morning visit to their patrons and greeted them with "Hail." That would get Vargunteius close enough to kill Cicero, who was the patron of many.

"What is that to me?" Cethegus asked.

"Yes, we may kill him in his bed, and safely," Vargunteius said.

Cethegus replied, "Safe is your way, then; take it. Mine's my own way."

He exited.

"Follow him, Vargunteius, and persuade him that the morning is the fittest time to kill Cicero," Catiline said.

"The night will turn all into riot, tumult, and turmoil," Longinus said.

"And perhaps fail to kill Cicero, too," Lentulus said.

Catiline said, "Entreat and plead with Cethegus in all our names —"

Lentulus added, "— by all our vows and friendships."

Vargunteius exited.

Sempronia, Aurelia, and Fulvia entered the room.

Sempronia asked, "Has our council broken up first?"

"You say that women are the greatest talkers," Aurelia said.

Aurelia whispered with Catiline, while Fulvia took Curius aside.

"We have finished our discussion and are now fit for action," Sempronia said.

"Which is passion. There's your best activity, lady," Longinus said.

Sempronia had a reputation for licentiousness.

"How does your wise Fatness know that?" Sempronia asked.

Longinus, who was fat, replied, "Your mother's daughter taught me, madam."

"Come, Sempronia, leave him alone," Catiline said. "He is a joker. And our present business is of more serious consequence and importance. Aurelia tells me you've done most masculinely — vigorously — within, and you have played the orator."

Sempronia said, "But we must hasten to execute our plot as well, and not remain inactive out of anxiety about the future."

"You say well, lady," Catiline said.

"I like our plot exceedingly well," Sempronia said. "It is sure to succeed, and we shall leave little to luck in it."

Catiline said to her, "Your banquet awaits you."

He then said, "Aurelia, take her in."

Looking around, he asked, "Where's Fulvia?"

Seeing Fulvia with Curius, Sempronia said, "Oh, the two lovers are coupling."

"Indeed, she's very ill from sitting up late," Curius said.

"You'd have her laugh and lie down," Sempronia said.

She was making a bawdy joke.

"Laugh and Lie Down" was the name of a card game.

Fulvia said, "No, indeed, Sempronia, I am not well. I'll take my leave; it draws close to the morning. Curius shall stay with you."

She then said to Aurelia, "Madam, I ask you to pardon me. I must consider my health."

"Farewell, good Fulvia," Aurelia said.

Whispering to Fulvia, Curius said, "Make haste and tell Cicero to get his guards about him. For Vargunteius and Cornelius have undertaken to murder him if Cethegus should miss. Their reason is that they think Cethegus' open rashness will permit easier discovery than their attempt, which will be veiled under friendship."

He said out loud to her, "I'll take you to your coach."

Whispering, he said, "Tell him also about Caesar's coming here earlier."

"My sweet madam, are you leaving?" Catiline asked.

"In truth, my lord, I have some indisposition," Fulvia said.

"I do wish you had all your health, sweet lady," Catiline replied.

He then said, "Lentulus, you'll do her service."

"I'll take her to her coach, and I'll give her the service due to her," Lentulus replied.

Everyone except Catiline exited.

Alone, Catiline said to himself:

"What agents men must use in their scheming!

"The rash, ambitious, needy, desperate, foolish, and wretched, even the dregs of mankind, all the way down to whores and women!

"Still, it must be so. Each has his or her own proper place, and they are the best in their jobs. Men-servants are fittest to kindle fires; slaves carry burdens, butchers are for slaughters; and apothecaries, wine-serving butlers, and cooks are for poisons.

"And so are these for me: dull, stupid Lentulus is my stale — my decoy — with whom I stalk and hunt; the rash Cethegus is my executioner; and fat Longinus, Statilius, Curius, Ceparius, and Cimber are my laborers, my pioneers who dig trenches, and they are my incendiaries."

A stale is a decoy. Hunters would keep an animal in front of them in order to get close to their prey.

Incendiaries are weapons that start fires.

Catiline continued:

"With these, I have domestic traitors, bosom thieves whom custom has called wives, the readiest helps to betray heady — impetuous and headstrong — husbands, to rob those who are at ease and lend the money in exchange for lust."

The wives rob the husbands and "lend" — give — the money to their lovers.

Catiline continued:

"Shall Catiline not do now, with these aids, so sought, so sorted — so recruited and given orders — something that shall be called their labor but his profit?

"And shall Catiline not make Caesar repent his advice to be bold to a spirit so much his lord and master in evil?

"Shall Caesar repent his advice when all these shall, like the brethren sprung of dragons' teeth, ruin each other, and he shall fall — die — among them with Crassus, Pompey, or whoever else appears even if they only resemble or are near a great one?"

Ancient mythology has tales of the sowing of dragon's teeth, leading to the growth of armed men who fight and kill each other.

Catiline continued:

"May my brain dissolve to water and my blood turn to phlegm, may my hands drop off, unworthy of my sword, and may that sword be inspired of itself to rip my breast for my lost entrails, when I leave a soul who will not serve me."

This society believed that the mixture of four humors in the body determined one's temperament. One humor could be predominant. The four humors are blood, yellow bile, black bile, and phlegm. If blood is predominant, then the person is sanguine (active, optimistic). If yellow bile is predominant, then the person is choleric (bad-tempered). If black bile is predominant, then the person is melancholic (sad). If phlegm is predominant, then the person is phlegmatic (calm, apathetic, indolent).

Catiline was optimistic that his rebellion would succeed.

Catiline continued:

"And those who will serve me are the same as with slaves: Such clay I am so bold as not to fear."

Catiline had no loyalty to his co-conspirators. Once they had served his needs, they would be tossed aside.

Catiline continued:

"The cruelty I mean to act I wish should be called mine and remain in my name, while after-ages do work themselves out in thinking to do the like but do it less. People in the future will try to be as evil as I am, but they shall fail.

"And even if in the future the power of all the fiends were let loose, with Fate to boot, my cruelty should be still the outstanding example.

"Soon what the Gauls or Moors could not effect — enduring victory over Rome — nor rival Carthaginians with their long history of spite and malice against Rome, shall be the work of one, and that my, night."

Rome and Carthage battled for supremacy in the Mediterranean. They fought three wars, each of which Rome won. The Punic Wars, also called the Carthaginian Wars, were fought between 264 and 146 B.C.E. Following the Third Carthaginian War, Rome completely destroyed Carthage.

— 3.4 —

Cicero and Fulvia talked together. A servant was present.

Cicero said to Fulvia, "I thank your vigilance."

He then said to the servant, "Where's my brother, Quintus? Call all my servants up."

The servant exited.

Cicero then said to Fulvia, "Tell noble Curius and say it to yourself: You are my saviors. But that's too little for you: You are Rome's saviors, too. Since you are Rome's saviors, what could I then hope less than that you be my saviors, too?"

Quintus entered the room.

Cicero said to his brother, "Oh, brother, now the engineers of the plot I told you about are working; the machinations begin to move. Where are your weapons? Arm all my household immediately. And order the porter not to let any man in until daytime."

"Not even your clients and your friends?" Quintus asked.

"The men who come to murder me wear those names," Cicero said. "They will pretend to be my clients and my friends. Yet send for Cato and Quintus Catulus — those men I dare to trust — and send for Flaccus and Pomtinius, the Praetors, by the back way."

Quintus said to Cicero, "Take care, good brother Marcus, that your fears are not formed greater than they should be. If they are, they will make your friends grieve while your enemies laugh."

Many people at the time thought that Cicero was exaggerating any dangers facing Rome and also exaggerating his heroic response to them.

Cicero replied, "It is a brother's counsel, and worth thanks. But do as I entreat you to do. I am exercising foresight, and I do not fear what people think about it."

Quintus exited.

Cicero asked Fulvia, "Was Caesar there, do you say?"

"Curius says he met him coming from there," Fulvia replied.

"Oh, so it's true," Cicero said. "And you had a council of ladies, too? Who was your speaker, madam?"

Fulvia answered, "She who would be the speaker, even if there had been forty more women there: Sempronia, who had both her Greek and her rhetorical figures of speech, and ever and anon — again and again — would ask us if the witty Consul could have improved on that, or if the orator Cicero could have said it better?"

The witty Consul was Cicero; in this society, "witty" meant "intelligent."

"She's my gentle enemy," Cicero said. "I wish that Cethegus had no more danger in him than she has! But my guards are you, great powers, and the unabated strengths of a firm conscience, which shall arm each step taken for the state and teach me to slack no pace for fear of malice."

The great powers could be great armies, the great gods, or both.

Quintus returned.

"How are things now, brother?" Cicero asked.

"Cato and Quintus Catulus were coming to you, and Crassus with them. I have let them in through the garden."

"What would Crassus want?" Cicero asked himself.

He was not entirely sure whether Crassus was a friend or an enemy. Crassus had sometimes been critical of him.

Quintus said, "I hear some people whispering by the gate and wondering whether it is too early, or not. But I think they are your friends and clients, and they are afraid to disturb you."

"You will change to another thought soon," Cicero said. "Have you given the porter the order I told you to give to him?"

"Yes," Quintus said.

"Withdraw and listen carefully," Cicero said.

They were going to listen to the would-be assassins who wanted to murder Cicero. Cicero wanted witnesses.

Vargunteius, Cornelius, and some armed men stood in front of Cicero's door.

"The door's not yet open," Vargunteius said.

"It would be best for you to knock," Cornelius said.

"Let the other assassins stand hidden nearby then and, when we are in, rush after us," Vargunteius said.

"But where's Cethegus?" Cornelius asked.

"He has quit the assassination, since he might not do it his way," Vargunteius said.

Vargunteius knocked.

The porter asked from inside the house, "Who's there?"

"A friend, or more," Vargunteius said.

He may have meant: 1) more than one friend, or 2) more than a friend — a client.

"I may not let any man in until daylight," the porter said.

"No? Why?" Vargunteius asked.

"What is your reason?" Cornelius asked.

"I am commanded so," the porter answered.

"By whom?" Vargunteius asked.

Cornelius said to the conspirators, "I hope that our plot has not been discovered."

"Yes, by betrayal," Vargunteius said to Cornelius.

He then asked the porter, "Please, good slave, who has commanded you?"

"He who may best command me — the Consul," the porter replied.

Cicero, Cato, Catulus, Crassus, and Quintus stood on a balcony and observed the scene.

"We are his friends," Vargunteius said.

The porter said, "All's one. It's all the same. It makes no difference."

"It is best that you tell him your name," Cornelius said to Vargunteius.

"Do you hear, fellow? I have some urgent business with the Consul. My name is Vargunteius."

Cicero spoke to them from above, using the third person, "True, he knows it, and he knows for what 'friendly' job you have been sent to do."

He then asked, "Cornelius, too, is there?"

"We are betrayed!" Vargunteius said to Cornelius.

"And desperate Cethegus, isn't he there?" Cicero asked.

Vargunteius said to Cornelius, "You speak. Cicero knows my voice. He will recognize it."

Cicero asked, "What do you say in answer to my question?"

"You are deceived, sir," Cornelius said.

Cicero said:

"No, it is you who are deceived, poor, misled men. Your states are yet worth pity, if you would listen and change your savage minds. Cease to be mad: Forsake your purposes of treason, rapine, murder, fire, and horror.

"The commonwealth has eyes that keep watch as vigilantly over her life as yours do for her — the commonwealth's — ruin.

"Be not deceived into thinking her lenity will be perpetual or, if men should be lacking, then the gods will be, to such a calling cause — the advocate of Rome against those who would hurt her."

The calling cause is a case that is called to justice. The gods would prosecute people who were traitors to Rome.

Cicero continued:

"Consider your assaults and, while there's time, repent them. It makes me tremble that there should yet breathe those spirits that, when they cannot live honestly, would rather perish basely."

Cato said to Marcus Tullius Cicero, "You talk too much to them, Marcus. They are lost. Go forth and apprehend them."

Catulus said to Cicero, "If you have proof of this piece of treachery, what should stop the commonwealth from taking due vengeance?"

Vargunteius said to the conspirators, "Let us slip away. The darkness has concealed us; we'll say some people have abused and misused our names."

Cornelius said, "We shall deny it all."

Vargunteius, Cornelius, and the other would-be assassins exited.

Cato said, "Quintus, what guards do you have? Call for the Tribunes' aid and wake up the city. Consul, you are too mild: The foulness of some evil deeds takes away all mercy. Report it to the Senate."

Suddenly, thunder sounded and lightning flashed violently.

"Listen," Cato said. "The gods grow angry with your patience. It is their concern, and it must be yours, that guilty men do not escape. As crimes grow, justice should rouse itself."

CHORUS (End of Chapter 3)

Blaming ambition for Rome's crisis, the Chorus said:

"What is it, Heavens, you prepare with so much swiftness and so sudden uprising? There are no Sons of Earth — no Giants and Titans — that dare again to rebellion, or to ambush the gods?

"The world shakes and nature fears, yet the tumult and the horror are greater within our minds than in our ears, so much do Rome's faults, now grown to be her fate, threaten her.

"The priests and people run about; each social class, age, and sex is terror-stricken at the others; and at the city-gates all are thronging out, as if their safety were to quit and leave their mother — Rome.

"Yet they find the same dangers there from which they make such haste to be preserved. For guilty states do ever bear the afflictions and calamities about them that they have deserved.

"And until those plagues rise above the mountain of our faults and there sit, we see them not. Thus still we love the evil we do until we suffer for or from it.

"But ambition, that vice which is close to virtue, has the fate of Rome most provoked and occasioned, and has now caused Rome herself to be not enough ransom to free her from the death with which she's yoked, that restless ill that always builds upon success and does not end, but begins, in aspiring.

"And ambition never is satiated while anything remains that seems even worth desiring, wherein the thought, unlike the eye, to which far things seem smaller than they are, deems all contentment placed on high, and thinks there's nothing great but what is far.

"Oh, Rome did not calculate her errors in time to forestall this fortune! If only Rome could have seen her crimes before they were past and had felt her faults before her punishment."

CHAPTER 4

— 4.1 —

The ambassadors of the Allobroges, who were tribesmen from Gaul, spoke together.

Thunder sounded and lightning flashed violently as several Senators, quaking and trembling, ran by them. To the Senators, the thunderstorm was an ominous warning of bad things to come.

An Allobrox said:

"Can these men be afraid, who are not only our masters but the world's masters? Then I see the gods reproach Rome for our sufferings, or the gods would humble these Senators, by sending them these frights while we are here, so that we might laugh at their ridiculous fear — the ridiculous fear of those whose names we trembled at beyond the Alps.

"Of all who pass, I do not see a face worthy a man who dares to look up and endure the sight of even one thunderbolt to the end with bravery; but they all look downward, like beasts, running away from every flash that is made. Even the end of the world could not deserve such timidity."

Men look up to the heavens; beasts look down to the ground.

The Allobrox continued:

"Are we employed here by our miseries, like superstitious fools, or rather slaves, to complain about our griefs, wrongs, and oppressions to a mere clothed Senate — their authority lies only in their clothing — whom our folly has made, and still intends to keep, our tyrants?

"It is our base petitionary breath that inflates them to this greatness, which this prick" — he drew his sword — "would soon let out, if we were at the same time both boldly brave and miserably wretched.

"When they have taken all we have — our goods, crops, lands, and houses — they will leave us this: a weapon and an arm that will still be found, although left naked, and whose status is lower than the ground."

It is wise not to outrage a subjugated people who have been robbed of gold and silver but who still have weapons.

Cato, Catulus, and Cicero entered the scene. All of them were Roman Senators.

Cato said, "Do, still present your anger, good and just heaven! Tell guilty men what powers are above them! In such a self-confidence and boldness arising from wickedness, it was time they should know something fit to fear."

He wanted the thunderstorm to continue. It was ominous, but only for traitors.

"I never saw a morning fuller of horror," Catulus said.

"To Catiline and his men," Cato said. "But to just men, although heaven should speak with all his wrath at once, with the result that with his breath the hinges of the world cracked, we should stand upright and unafraid."

"Why, so we do, good Cato," Cicero said.

Seeing the ambassadors, he asked, "Who are these men?"

"I take them to be ambassadors from the Allobroges, judging by their clothing," Catulus said.

An Allobrox said to his fellow ambassadors, "Aye, these men seem to be of a different race than the frightened Romans we just saw. Let's seek justice from these men. There's hope of justice, with their fortitude and bravery."

The Allobroges approached the Senators.

Cicero said to the Allobrogian ambassadors, "Friends of the Senate and of Rome, today we ask you to leave us alone. Tomorrow what suit you have, given to us by Fabius Sanga, whose patronage your state has and uses, just know by the Consul's — that is, my own — word, you shall receive either a quick reply or else an answer worth your patience."

Fabius Sanga was the patron of the Allobroges; he was in effect their Roman-citizen ambassador who represented their interests in Rome. Fabius Sanga was a descendant of Fabius Allobrogicus, who had conquered the tribe. Traditionally, the conqueror of a tribe would become their patron. That patronage would be passed down in the family.

The Allobrox said, "We could not hope for more, most worthy Consul."

Cato, Catulus, and Cicero exited.

The Allobrox said to his fellow ambassadors:

"This magistrate has struck an awe into me and by his sweetness has won a greater regard for his official position than all the boisterous dispositions that ignorant greatness employs to fill the large, ill-fitting authority it wears.

"How easy is a noble spirit recognized as being different from the harsh and sulfurous matter that flies out in harsh, contumelious language, makes a noise, and stinks!

"May we find good and great men who know how to condescend to consider wants and fitting necessities, and who will not turn away from any fair suits.

"Such men don't help the cause they undertake with favor and success more than, by doing so, they raise their own good reputations by turning just men's needs into praise of themselves because of their just actions."

By doing the right thing, good and great people get praise heaped on them. It's a win-win situation for the people whom they help and for the good and great themselves.

Some Lictors, a Praetor, Marcus Tullius Cicero, Antonius, Cato, Catulus, Caesar, Crassus, and the other Senators entered the temple of Jupiter *Stator* for a meeting that Cicero had called after the assassination attempt against him had failed.

"Make room for the Consuls!" the Praetor called. "Fathers, take your places."

The "Fathers" were Senators. Sometimes, they were called conscript Fathers. The word "conscript" means enrolled or elected. Conscript Fathers are those men who are enrolled or elected into the Roman Senate.

The Praetor continued, "Here, in the house of Jupiter the Stayer, by edict from the Consul Marcus Tullius, you are met, a full, well-attended Senate. Hear him speak."

Jupiter was known as Jupiter *Stator*, the stayer, maintainer, and supporter of Rome.

Marcus Tullius Cicero began:

"I wish what may be happy and auspicious always to Rome and hers. Honored and conscript — elected — Fathers, if I were silent, and if all the dangers threatening the state and you were yet so hidden in the night or darkness that is thicker in the breasts of those who are the black contrivers, so that no beam of light could pierce them and reveal them, yet the voice of heaven — the thunder — this morning spoke loudly enough to give you a feeling of the horror and awaken you from a sleep as stark and rigid as death.

"I have recently spoken often in this Senate concerning this topic, but I always have lacked either your ears or your faith because their plots have seemed so incredible, or I have seemed so vain as to make up these things for my own glory and false greatness, as rumor has it. But so be it.

"When the dangers break forth and shall declare themselves by their too foul results, then the unpopularity of my just cares will find another name.

"As for me, I am just one person; and this poor life, so recently aimed at in an assassination attempt not an hour yet since, they cannot with more eagerness pursue my life than I with gladness would lay down and lose it to buy Rome's peace, if that would purchase it.

"But when I see they'd make the loss of my life only the step to more and greater losses, all the way to the loss of your lives, Rome's lives, all lives, I would with those lives preserve it, or then fall and die as part of Rome's destruction."

Julius Caesar and Crassus talked apart from the others present.

Caesar said:

"Aye, aye, leave it to you alone, cunning artificer — trickster!

"See how his gorget — his throat-armor — appears and peers out above his gown, to tell the people in what danger he was.

"Vargunteius acted absurdly when he named himself before he got into Cicero's home."

Crassus said, "It doesn't matter, as long as they deny it all and can just maintain the same lie constantly and steadfastly."

He then asked, "Will Catiline be here?"

"I've sent for him," Caesar said.

"And have you told him to be confident?" Crassus asked.

"To that his own necessity will prompt him," Caesar said.

"Seem to believe nothing at all that Cicero relates to us," Crassus said.

"It will madden him," Caesar said.

"Oh, and help the other faction," Crassus said.

Cicero's brother, Quintus, entered and conferred with him.

Crassus asked, "Who is that? His brother? What new intelligence has he brought him now?"

The intelligence — news — included the information that Quintus had brought some guards to protect Cicero.

Caesar said, "He has brought him some cautions from his wife about how to behave himself."

Cicero said to Quintus, "Place some of the guards outside, and bring some inside. Thank their kind loves."

Quintus exited.

Cicero then said to the Senate, "It is a comfort yet that all do not abandon their country's cause."

Quintus returned, bringing in the Tribunes and some guards.

Caesar whispered to Antonius, who had been elected Consul with Cicero, "What is this now? What is the meaning of this muster, Consul Antonius?"

"I do not know," Antonius said. "Ask my colleague Cicero. He'll tell you. There is some reason in state that I must yield to, and I have promised him — indeed, he has bought it, by giving me the province of Macedonia."

Now that the guards were present, Cicero spoke about Catiline without naming him:

"I acknowledge that it grieves me, Fathers, that I am compelled to draw these arms and aids for your defense, and, more, I must draw them against a citizen of Rome, born here among you, a patrician, a man, I must confess, of no low family nor no small virtue, if he had employed those excellent gifts of fortune and of nature to the good, not ruin, of the state.

"But being bred in his father's needy fortunes, he advanced his position politically by prostituting his sister, and he confirmed his position with civil slaughter, entering first into the politics of the commonwealth with murders of some of the gentry while he was a follower of Sulla.

"He has done these things by study, inclination, custom, and habit, and he is familiar with all licentiousness. What could be hoped for in such a field of riot and an expanse of debauchery, but a course of action that is extremely pernicious?

"Although, I must avow, I found his evils sooner with my eyes than with my thought, and I found his evils with these hands of mine before they touched at my suspicion."

Catiline's evils were so great that Cicero could not believe them although he saw them — and felt them.

Julius Caesar, who knew that Cicero was speaking about Catiline, said, "What are his evil deeds, Consul? You declaim against his behavior and corrupt your own."

Caesar then stated a maxim: "No wise man should out of hatred of guilty men lose his own innocence."

Cicero responded:

"The noble Caesar speaks godlike truth.

"But when he [Caesar] hears I can convict him [Catiline] by his [Catiline's] behavior in his [Catiline's] evil deeds, he [Caesar] might be silent, and not cast away his [Caesar's] sentences — his [Caesar's] maxims — in vain where they scarcely apply to his [Caesar's] subject."

Catiline entered the scene.

Cato said, "Here he himself comes."

Catiline sat down by Cato, who stood up and moved away because he was unwilling to sit by him.

Cato said, "If Catiline is worthy of any good man's voice and vote, then that good man can sit down by him; Cato will not."

Catulus, who was sitting by Catiline, stood up and said, "If Cato leaves him, I'll not keep by his side."

Other Senators also moved away from Catiline.

"What face and appearance is this that the Senate here assumes against me, Fathers?" Catiline asked. "Allow my modesty and sense of honor and propriety to ask the cause of so much coldness."

Julius Caesar said to Lucius Sergius Catiline, "It is reported here that you are the head of a hostile faction, Lucius."

"Aye," Cicero said, "and that accusation will be proved against him."

Catiline rose from his seat and said:

"So let it be.

"Why, Consul, if in the commonwealth, there should be two bodies, one lean, weak, rotten, and has a head, while the other is strong and healthful, but has no head, if I give it a head, do I offend?"

The Senators made known their displeasure at hearing this.

Catiline continued:

"Restore yourselves to your good temper, Fathers, and without perturbation hear me speak. Remember who I am, and of what place and position, and remember what petty fellow this is who opposes me. He is one who has exercised his eloquence always to the bane of the nobility, a boasting, insolent tongue-man."

Cicero was a member of the equestrian class, just below the level of the Senatorial class, which was dominated by nobles. The basis for the equestrian class was economic. Cicero's name came from the Latin word for chickpea: *cicer*. Most likely, his ancestors sold chickpeas.

"Be silent, evil traitor, or wash your mouth," Cato said. "Cicero is an honest man and loves his country. I wish that you did, too."

"Cato, you are too zealous for him," Catiline said.

"No, you are too impudent," Cato said.

"Catiline, be silent," Catulus said.

"Nay," Catiline said, "for then I easily fear that my just defense will come too late, with so much prejudice against me."

Julius Caesar asked himself, "Will he sit down?"

He was wondering what Catiline would do: stand up for himself, or the opposite.

"Let the world forsake me," Catiline said, "yet my innocence must not."

"You innocent?" Cato said. "Then so are the furies."

In this context, the furies are violently angry mortals whose anger approaches madness.

Cicero said, "Yes, and Atë, too."

Atë is a goddess who causes human beings to act rashly — in such a way that it causes their destruction.

Cicero continued:

"Don't you blush, pernicious Catiline? Or has the paleness caused by your guilt drunk up your blood and drawn your veins as dry of blood as your heart is dry of truth and your breast is dry of virtue?

"How long, then, will you abuse our patience?

"Shall your fury always mock us? To what licentiousness and disregard of law does your unbridled boldness dare run itself?

"Do all the nightly guards kept on the palace — the Palatine Hill — the city's watches, with the people's fears, the rallying of all good citizens, this so strong and fortified seat, here, of the Senate, that presently looks upon you, impress you not at all?

"Don't you feel your plans all laid open, and see your wild conspiracy restrained by each man's knowledge of it? Which of all this order can you think ignorant — if they'll but utter their conscience and inward conviction rightly — of what you did last night, what on the former, where you were, whom you called together, what your plots were?

"Oh, the times and manners!

"This the Consul sees, the Senate understands, yet this man lives! Lives, aye, and comes here into council with us, participates in our discussion about public cares and concerns, and with his eye marks and designates each man of us to slaughter.

"And we good men think we satisfy the state and do our duty, if we can shun just this man's sword and madness."

The word "shun" can mean 1) loathe, 2) flee from, 3) evade, and 4) avoid.

Cicero's point was that action — more action than mere shunning — was needed. The Senators thought that they were good men, but they were actually doing very little to help Rome.

Cicero continued:

"There was that virtue once in Rome when good men would with more sharp coercion and application of force have restrained a wicked citizen than the deadliest foe.

"We have that law still, Catiline, for you. The Senate has passed an act that is as grave and authoritative as it is sharp. The Republic does not lack the law, nor does this Senate lack the authority to enforce it.

"We, we who are Consuls, only we ourselves fail — we are the ones who are lacking.

"For twenty days now we have let grow dull and rust the edge of that decree giving Consuls absolute authority to act. We have kept it shut up, as in a sheath, which when drawn should take your head.

"Yet you still live, and you live not to lay aside your audacity arising from wickedness, but to confirm it.

"I could desire, Fathers, to be found still merciful, to seem, in these great perils grasping the state, a man remiss and slack. But then I should condemn myself as being guilty of sloth and treachery.

"Their military camp is in Italy, pitched and set up in the jaws — the narrow passes — of Etruria, their numbers daily increasing and their general within our walls, nay in our council, plotting hourly some fatal evil to the public.

Etruria is in central Italy. Catiline's army was close to Florence, which was in Etruria. Rome is south of Etruria.

Cicero continued:

"If, Catiline, I should command you now here to be taken and killed, I justifiably wonder whether all good men would not think it done rather too late than any man too cruel."

"Except he were of the same type of flour and batch of loaves," Cato said.

He meant: Unless he were the same sort of man as Catiline.

Cicero continued:

"But that which ought to have been done long since, I will, and for good reason, yet forbear from doing.

"Then I will take you, when no man is found so lost, so wicked, indeed, so like yourself, but shall profess that it is done out of need, and out of right.

"While there is one who dares to defend you, Catiline, live on.

"You shall have leave, but you will live as you now live. You are and will be watched closely, besieged, and suppressed from working the smallest disturbance and civil unrest to the state.

"I have those eyes and ears that shall always keep guard and spy on you, as they have always done, and you will not feel it nor be aware of it.

"What then can you hope for? Neither night can with her darkness hide your wicked meetings, nor a private house can in her walls contain the guilty whispers of your conspiracy. If all breaks out, all will be revealed, so change your mind at last, and lose your thoughts of ruin, flame, and slaughter.

"Remember how I told to the Senate here that on such a day your Lictor, Caius Manlius, would be in arms. Was I deceived, Catiline, either in the fact, or in the time, the hour?"

Manlius had raised an army for Catiline.

Cicero continued:

"I said, too, in this Senate that your purpose was on the fifth of the Kalends of November [October 28; the fifth day before the first of November, counting November first as one day], to have slaughtered this whole order of leading citizens. This warning of mine made many leave the city.

"Can you here deny that your black design was hindered that very day by me, with yourself closed in within my protecting forces, so that you could not move against a public decree and against a republic?

"When you were heard to say, upon the parting of the rest, that you would content yourself with the murder of us who remained?

"Hadn't you hope, besides, by an ambush by night to take Praeneste?"

Praeneste was a stronghold approximately twenty miles south-east of Rome.

Cicero continued:

"Where, when you came, didn't you find the place secured and fortified against you with my aids, my watches? My garrisons fortified it.

"You do nothing, Sergius. You can endeavor to do nothing, nay, you cannot think, but I both see and hear your thought, and I am with you, by, and before, about, and in you, too.

"Just remember your last night's business. Come, I'll use no circumlocution: I will speak plainly.

"Remember Laeca's house, the workshop and foundry of your conspiracy, among your sword-men, where so many associates both of your evil and your madness met.

"Dare you deny this? Why are you silent?

"Speak and deny it, and this shall convict you and find you guilty: Here they are, I see them, in this Senate, those who were with you.

"Oh, you immortal gods, in what region of the earth are we? What region do we live in? In what air? What commonwealth or state is this we have?

"Here, here, among us, among our own number, Fathers, in this most holy council of the world, are men who seek the destruction of me, of you, of ours, of all.

"What I can name and specify is too narrow and too limited: Follow the sun around the world, and nowhere will you find ambition to rival theirs.

"As Consul, I behold these men. Indeed, I ask for their advice concerning the state, as I would as though I were asking advice from good patriots.

"Those whom it would be fitting for the axe to hew in pieces, I not so much as wound yet with my voice.

"You were last night with Laeca, Catiline. Your shares of Italy you and your co-conspirators there divided, and you appointed who and to where each should go.

"What men should stay behind in Rome were chosen, your tasks were set down, the parts and places of the city were marked out to be set on fire.

"You yourself, you affirmed, were ready to depart. Only a little hindrance held you back: The hindrance was that I yet lived.

"Upon the word stepped forth three of your crew to rid you of that care. Two undertook this morning, before day, to kill me in my bed.

"All this I knew when your meeting was scarcely broken up. I armed all my servants, called both my brother and friends, shut out your followers you sent to visit me, whose names I told to some witnesses with me there, of high rank, before your followers came to my house."

"Yes, both Quintus Catulus and I can affirm it," Cato said.

Caesar said to himself about Catiline, "He's lost and gone. His spirits have forsaken him."

The spirits could be Catiline's guardian spirits or his psychological spirits, or both.

Cicero continued:

"If this is so, why, Catiline, why do you stay? Go where you mean to go. The ports are open. Go forth!

"The military camp abroad has lacked you, their chief, too long. Lead all your troops out with you. Purge the city. Draw dry that noisome and pernicious cesspool — your followers — who, left behind in Rome, would infect the world."

Cicero wanted all of Catiline's co-conspirators to leave Rome. That would not happen.

Cicero continued:

"You will free me of all my fears at once, once I see a city-wall between us. Do you give up the idea of doing that thing now, commanded by me, which before of your own choice you were prone to do? Go! The Consul tells you, an enemy, to depart from the city.

"'Whither?' you will ask. 'To exile?' I do not tell you that. But if you ask me for my counsel, I will advise you to go into exile.

"What is there here in Rome that can delight you? In Rome, where there is not a soul outside your own foul cluster of associates but fears and hates you?

"What domestic brand of private filthiness exists but that which is burnt into your life?

"What hidden and secret shame exists but that which has become part of your known infamy?

"What lust was ever absent from your eyes?

"What evil deed was ever absent from your hands?

"What wickedness was ever absent from your whole body?

"Where's that youth, drawn in within your nets or caught with your baits before whose rage you have not borne a sword, and to whose lusts you have not held a torch?

"Your latter nuptials — your marriage to Aurelia — I let pass in silence. In your latter nuptials, sins incredible on sins were heaped, which I will not name, lest in a civil state so monstrous facts should either be seen to have taken place or be seen to have not been punished.

"Your ruined finances, too, I glance not at. Your finances hang on and survive only until the next Ides."

The Ides was a day of payment of interest or debts. People without the money to pay their interest or debts would be ruined.

Cicero continued:

"I come to that which is more known, more public: the life and safety of us all, by you threatened and sought.

"Didn't you stand in the field of Campus Martius when Lepidus and Tullus were our old Consuls, upon the day of choice, armed and with forces to take the lives of the newly elected Consuls, and our chief citizens', when neither your fear nor your conscience changed your mind, and nothing but the fortunate luck of the commonwealth withstood your active malice?"

Cicero was referring to the first Catilinarian conspiracy.

Cicero continued:

"Speak the truth.

"How often have you attempted to take my life? How many of your assaults have I avoided only by moving my body out of the path of the dagger, as we'd say, and wresting your dagger from your hand? How often? How often has the dagger fallen or slipped by chance?"

Cicero had figuratively, not literally, moved his body out of the path of the dagger and wrested it from Catiline's hand.

Cicero continued:

"Yet doesn't the sheath at your side want your dagger back again? I don't know which vows you have made to the dagger or with what rites you have consecrated it to yourself, with the result that you still make it a necessity to stab it in the body of a Consul."

In other words, Catiline kept wanting to stab and kill Cicero.

Cicero continued:

"But let me stop this way of speaking and speak to you not as one moved by hatred, which is how I ought to speak to you, but as one who is moved by pity, of which none is owing to you."

"No more than is owing to Tantalus or Tityus," Cato said.

Tantalus was so proud that he tried to fool the gods. He killed and cooked his own son, Pelops, and he put the meat into a stew that he served the gods. The gods knew the trick, however, so they did not eat the stew — with the exception of the goddess Demeter, who ate part of Pelops' shoulder. Outraged, the gods brought Pelops to life again and gave him a shoulder made out of ivory, and they sentenced Tantalus to eternal torment in the Land of the Dead. He stands in a stream of water, and branches heavily laden with ripe fruit are overhead, yet Tantalus is eternally thirsty and hungry. Whenever Tantalus bends over to drink from the stream, the water dries up. Whenever Tantalus reaches overhead to seize a piece of fruit, a breeze blows the fruit just out of his reach.

Tityus had once kidnapped and tried to rape Leto, the consort of Jupiter and mother of Apollo and Diana. For this infamous deed, Tityus, whose giant body lies across nine acres, is in Tartarus. Two vultures feed on his liver, which, once eaten, grow back so the vultures can eat it again and eternally torment Tityus.

Cicero continued:

"You came a short while ago into this Senate. Who in such a crowd of people, with so many friends and kindred you have here, saluted you?

"Weren't the seats made bare upon your entrance? Didn't the Consular men — Senators who are ex-Consuls — rise and leave their places, as soon as you sat down, and fled your side as if you were a plague or a ruin, knowing how often they had been by you marked out for the slaughterhouse?

"How do you bear this? Surely, if my slaves at home feared me with half the fright and horror that here your fellow citizens fear you, I would soon quit my house and think it necessary, too.

"Yet you dare to tarry here? Go forth at last, condemn yourself to flight and solitude. Discharge the commonwealth of her deep fear. Go. Go into banishment, if this is the word you have been waiting for.

"Why do you look around you? They all consent to it. Do you await the authority of their voices, whose silent wills condemn you? While they sit, they approve it; while they allow it, they decree it; and while they are silent to it, they proclaim it.

"If you prove yourself there honest and free from reproach, I'll endure the envy.

"But there's no thought you should ever be he whom either shame should call from filthiness, terror should call from danger, or reason should call from fury.

"Go, I entreat you — yet why do I so, when I already know they have been sent ahead and tarry for you in arms and expect you on the Aurelian Way?"

The Aurelian Way went from Rome north along the western coast and into Etruria, where Catiline's troops were located.

Marcus Tullius Cicero continued:

"I know the day agreed between you and Manlius, to whom the silver eagle, too, is sent before, which I hope shall prove to you as baneful as you imagine it to the commonwealth.

"But this wise and sacred Senate may say: 'What do you mean, Marcus Tullius? If you know that Catiline is awaited to be chief of a civil war and you know that he's the author of such a wickedness, the summoner of well-known evil men to an action of so much horror, the leader of such a treason, then why do you send him forth? Why let him escape? This is to give him liberty and power. Instead, you should lay hold upon him and send him to a deserved death and a just punishment.'

"To these so holy voices, thus I answer: If I did think it timely, conscript Fathers, to punish him with death, I would not give the fencer the use of one short hour to breathe."

The fencer is a swordsman, a gladiator. Gladiators were prisoners of war, or they were slaves. To call someone a fencer was an insult.

Cicero continued:

"But when there are in this grave order — the Senate — some who with weak judgments still nurse his hopes, some who, with not believing, have confirmed his designs more, and whose authority the weaker men, as well as the worst men, have followed, I would now send him where they all should see, clear as the light, his heart shine, his intentions made clear; where no man could be so wickedly or foolishly stupid, but should cry out he saw, touched, felt, and grasped it.

"Then, when he has run out himself, led forth his desperate party with him, collected aids of all kinds, both shipwrecked minds and fortunes, not only the grown evil that now has sprung and sprouted forth would be plucked up and weeded, but also the stock, root, and seed of all the evils choking the commonwealth.

"Whereas, should we take only him out of such a swarm of traitors, our cares and fears might seem a while relieved, but the main peril would bide still enclosed deep in the veins and bowels of the state. As human bodies laboring with fevers, while they are caused to toss and turn with heat, if they do take cold water, seem for that short space much eased, but afterward are ten times more afflicted.

"Wherefore, I say, let all this wicked crew depart, divide themselves from good men, and gather their forces to one head. As I said often, let them be severed from us with a wall. Let them leave off assassination attempts upon the Consul in his own house, to surround the Praetor, to surround the court with weapons, to prepare fire and missiles, swords, torches, sulfur, firebrands. In short, let it be written on each man's forehead what thoughts he bears the public.

"I here promise, conscript Fathers, to you and to myself that diligence in us Consuls, for my honored colleague abroad and for myself at home."

Cicero's fellow Consul, Antonius, would lead the Roman army against Catiline's army.

Cicero continued:

"I here promise you so great authority in you, so much virtue in these, the gentlemen — *equites* — of Rome, whom I could scarcely restrain today in zeal from seeking out the parricide to slaughter."

Some of the *equites*, members of the upper class just below the Senatorial class, wanted to lynch Catiline.

Cicero continued:

"And I here promise you so much unanimity in all good men and minds as, only on Catiline's going out of Rome, all treachery shall be clear, made plain, oppressed, revenged."

Catiline was a parricide in the sense that he wanted to kill the leading citizens of Rome, including and especially Cicero, the leader of the opposition to him.

Cicero continued:

"And with this omen, this portent of the future, go, pernicious plague, out of the city, to the wished-for destruction of you and those who, to the ruin of her, have taken that bloody and black sacrament."

Cicero wanted Catiline — the pernicious plague — and his co-conspirators to leave Rome. The omen — the portent of the future —

was Cicero's speech and promises. The bloody and black sacrament was the drinking of the slave's blood mixed with wine.

Cicero continued:

"You, Jupiter, whom we call the Stayer — the Maintainer — both of this city and this empire, will, with the same auspice you did raise it first, drive from your altars and all other temples and buildings of this city, from our walls, lives, states, and fortunes of our citizens this fiend, this fury, with his accomplices.

"And all of this offence to good men — these known traitors to their country, thieves of Italy, joined in so damned a league of evil — you will with perpetual plagues, alive and dead, punish for Rome and save her innocent head."

Catiline responded:

"If an oration or highly wrought language, Fathers, could make me guilty, here is one — Cicero — who has done it. He has striven to emulate this morning's thunder with his prodigious rhetoric.

"But I hope that this Senate is more serious and dignified than to give credit rashly to all he vomits against a man of your own order, a patrician, and one whose ancestors have deserved more from Rome than this man's eloquence could utter, turned the best way, as always it is the worst."

Catiline was complaining that he deserved the best that could be spoken about him, yet Cicero always spoke the worst that could be said about him.

Cato said, "His eloquence has deserved more today, in speaking your ill, than all your ancestors did in their good. And the state that he has saved will find that fact to be true."

Catiline said, "Who, he? If I were that enemy that he would make me, I'd not wish the state more wretched than to need him to preserve it. What do you make him out to be, Cato? You make such a man as he out to be a Hercules? An Atlas? He is a poor petty inmate!"

Hercules is the great panhellenic hero.

Atlas is the Titan who holds up the sky.

Catiline was proud. He was against Cicero in part because Cicero was a member of the *equites* class, while Catiline was a member of the higher Senatorial class. In addition, Cicero was a mere inmate — lodger — in Rome, according to Catiline. He was not born in Rome, but instead was born in Arpinum and then came to Rome.

"Traitor!" Cato shouted.

"*He* save the state?" Catiline said. "A burgess' son of Arpinum? The gods would rather twenty Romes should perish than have that contumely — insult and disgrace — stuck upon them that he should share with them in the preserving a shed, or a sign-post."

"Shut up, you monster!" Cato shouted.

Catiline said, "The gods would be attacked themselves again, and lost in the first rude and indigested heap — the primal chaos — before such a wretched name as Cicero should sound with theirs."

"Away, you impudent person!" Catulus shouted.

"Do you all back him?" Catiline said. "Are you silent, too? Well, I will leave you, Fathers; I will go. But —"

He turned suddenly on Cicero.

He continued, "— my fine dainty speaker—"

Cicero interrupted, "What now, fury? Will you assault me here?"

"Help, aid the Consul!" the Chorus shouted.

Catiline said, "See, Fathers, don't you laugh? Who threatened him? In vain you conceive, ambitious orator, hope of so splendid a death as by this hand."

"Out of the court with the pernicious traitor!" Cato shouted. "Make him leave!"

Catiline said to Cicero, "There is no title that this flattering Senate, nor honor that the base multitude can give you, that shall make you worthy of Catiline's anger."

"Stop," Cato shouted. "Stop Catiline's monstrous mouth!"

Catiline said, "Or when it shall stop, I'll look at you, and my look shall kill you."

"Will no one restrain the monster?" Cato shouted.

"Parricide!" Catulus shouted.

Catiline was a parricide in that he wanted to kill Cicero. As Consul, Cicero was the head of his country, as a father is the head of a family in a paternalistic culture

"Butcher, traitor, leave the Senate!" Quintus shouted.

Catiline said, "I am going into banishment, to please you, Fathers. I am thrust headlong forth."

"Do you still murmur, monster?" Cato said.

Catiline said, "Since I am thus put out, and made a —"

"What?" Cicero interrupted.

"Not guiltier than you are," Catulus said.

Catiline said, "I will not burn without my funeral pyre."

"What does the fiend say?" Cato asked.

Catiline said, "I will have fuel, timber, to build my funeral pyre."

"Sing out, screech-owl," Cato said. "Sing out, bird of ill omen."

Catiline said, "It shall be in —"

"Speak your incomplete thoughts," Catullus interrupted.

Catiline continued, "— the common fire, rather than my own. For fall I will with all, before I fall alone."

Catiline exited.

Crassus said quietly to Caesar, "He's lost: There's no hope for him."

Caesar replied quietly, "Unless he immediately takes arms and gives a blow before the Consul's forces can be levied."

"What is your pleasure, Fathers?" Cicero asked. "What shall be done?"

"See that the commonwealth receives no loss," Catulus said.

"Commit the care thereof to the Consuls," Cato said.

Crassus said, "It is the time."

Caesar said, "And there is need."

Crassus and Caesar now at least publicly seemed to support Cicero.

Cicero said, "I give thanks to this frequent — full, well-attended — Senate. But what do they decree to Curius and Fulvia?"

Curius and Fulvia had informed on the conspiracy.

"What the Consul shall think suitable and fitting," Catulus said.

"They must receive reward, although it is not publicly known," Cicero said, "lest when a state needs ministers, the ministers will have no informers."

If informers are not rewarded, there will be few or no informers. The ministers of a state need informers to give them information on which they can act.

The Senators left, but Cato and Marcus Tullius Cicero stayed behind and talked privately.

Cato said, "Yet, Marcus Tullius, I believe that Crassus and this Caesar here ring hollow and are false to Rome."

Cicero replied, "And they would be proved to be so, if we dared to test them."

"Why don't we dare to test them?" Cato asked. "What honest act exists that the Roman Senate should not dare, and do?"

Cicero replied, "Not an unprofitable, dangerous act that would stir too many serpents up at once. Caesar and Crassus, if they are ill men, are mighty and powerful ones; and we must so provide that, while we take one head from this foul Hydra, twenty more heads do not grow."

"I approve your counsel," Cato said.

"They shall be watched, examined, and remembered," Cicero said. "Until they declare themselves, I will not put them out by any question. There they stand. I'll make myself no enemies, nor the state no traitors."

Catiline was still in Rome.

He, Lentulus, Cethegus, Curius, Gabinius, Longinus, and Statilius talked together.

Catiline said, "False to ourselves? All our designs revealed to this state-cat?"

A state-cat is a person carefully watching the state the way a cat carefully watches a mouse. In this case, the state-cat was Cicero.

"Aye, if I had had my way, he would have mewed in flames at home, not in the Senate," Cethegus said. "I had singed his furs by this time."

Catiline said:

"Well, there's now no time of retracting our former actions, or our standing still. We can't change what has passed.

"Friends, be yourselves; keep the same Roman hearts and ready minds that you had yesternight at Laeca's house. Prepare to execute what we resolved. And do not let labor or danger or discovery frighten you.

"I'll go to the army; you, in the meantime, make ready things here at home in Rome. Draw to you any aids that you think fit, of men of all conditions or any fortunes that may help in a war.

"I'll either bleed out my life-blood or win an empire for you.

"Within the next few days, look to see my battle flags here at the walls; be you but firm within.

"In the meantime, to cause dislike of the Consul and give less suspicion of our course of action, let it be given out here in the city that I, an innocent man, have gone into exile into Massilia, willing to bow to fate and the times, being unable to withstand so great a faction without troubling the commonwealth, whose peace I rather seek than all the glory of struggle or any action to vindicate my own innocence.

"Farewell, the noble Lentulus, Longinus, Curius, the rest — and you, my better genius — my attendant spirit — the brave Cethegus.

"When we meet again, we'll sacrifice to liberty."

"And revenge," Cethegus said, "so that we may praise our hands once."

Lentulus said, "Oh, you Fates, give Fortune now her eyes, to see with whom she visits, so that she may never forsake him!"

Lady Fortune is proverbially blind.

Curius said, "He does not need Lady Fortune, nor her eyes. Proceed, Sergius. A valiant man is his own fate and fortune."

"May the fate and fortune of us all go with him!" Longinus said.

"And always guard him!" Gabinius Statilius said.

"I am the obedient servant of all of you," Lucius Sergius Catiline said.

He exited.

Lentulus said:

"Now, friends, it is left with us. I have already dealt, by Umbrenus, with the Allobroges who are here resident in Rome, whose state I hear is discontent with the avarice and extortion of the governing magistrates they are oppressed with and by, and they have made diverse complaints to the Senate, but all in vain.

"These men I have thought — both for their own oppressions and also because, by nature, they are a people who are warlike and fierce, still seeking change and now hating our state — the fittest and the easiest to be drawn into our society of conspirators, and to aid the war. This is true all the more because of their geographical location — they border Italy — and because they abound with horses and cavalry, which is the one thing our military camp lacks.

"Also, I have found them forthcoming and inclined to help us. They will meet soon at Sempronia's house, where I would ask you all to be present, to greater confirm and strengthen their support for our cause. The sight of such high spirits as we have will be no harm, nor will our great number."

"I will not fail," Gabinius said.

"Nor I," Statilius said.

"Nor I," Curius said.

Cethegus said, "I wish that I had something by myself, apart from the others, to do. I have no spirit or inclination for these many councils. Let me kill all the Senate for my share. I'll do it at their next sitting."

"Worthy Caius, your presence at the meeting will add much," Lentulus said.

"I shall spoil more," Cethegus said.

Cicero and Fabius Sanga talked together. Sanga was a Roman Senator and the patron of the Allobroges.

Cicero said, "The state's beholden to you, Fabius Sanga, for this great care. And those Allobroges are more than wretched, if they lend a listening to such persuasion by the conspirators."

Sanga replied, "They, most worthy Consul, as men employed here from a grieved state, groaning beneath a multitude of wrongs, and being told there was small hope of ease to be expected to their evils from here, were willing at first to give an ear and listen to anything that spoke of liberty. But since then, because of better thoughts and my urged reasons, they have come about and won to the true side. The Fortune of the commonwealth has conquered."

"Who is that same Umbrenus, who was the intermediary between the conspirators and the Allobroges?" Cicero asked.

"One who has had business transactions in Gallia often and is known to their state," Sanga answered.

"Have the ambassadors come with you?" Cicero asked.

"Yes," Sanga answered.

"Well, bring them in," Cicero said. "If they are steadfast and honest, never have men had the opportunity so to justly deserve rewards from Rome as they have."

Sanga exited.

Alone, Cicero said to himself, "A happy, wished-for occasion, and thrust into my hands, for the discovery and manifestly proven conviction of these traitors. Be thanked, O Jupiter!"

Sanga returned with the ambassadors of the Allobroges.

Cicero said, "My worthy lords, allies by treaty of the Senate, you are welcome. I understand by Quintus Fabius Sanga, your painstaking patron here, you have been lately solicited against the commonwealth by a man named Umbrenus — take a seat, please —"

They sat.

Cicero continued:

"— who came to you from Publius Lentulus, who wants you to be associates in Catiline's and the other conspirators' intended war. I could caution you that men whose fortunes are yet flourishing, and are Rome's friends, would not without a good reason become her enemies and mix themselves and their estates with the lost hopes of Catiline or Lentulus, whose mere despair arms them.

"That would be to risk certain-to-happen good things for airy promises and to undergo all danger for a voice and a promise.

"Believe me, friends: Loud tumults are not laid down with half the easiness that they are raised up. All may begin a war, but few can end it.

"The Senate has decreed that my colleague — the other Consul, Antonius — shall lead the Senators' army against Catiline, and has declared both Catiline and Manlius traitors.

"Our Metellus Celer has already given part of their troops defeat. Honors are promised to all who will quit them, and rewards proposed even to slaves who can detect their courses of action and inform us about them.

"Here in the city of Rome I have, by the Praetors and Tribunes, placed my guards and watches so that not a foot can tread, not a breath can whisper, but I have knowledge of it.

"And be sure that the Senate and the people of Rome, out of their accustomed greatness, will sharply and severely punish not only any evil deed but any conspiracy or purpose against the state.

"Therefore, my lords, consult of your own ways, and think which direction is best for you to take. You, now, are present suitors for some redress of wrongs: I'll undertake not only that that redress shall be assured you, but also whatever grace or privilege else the Senate or Roman people can cast upon you that is worthy such a service as you have now the way and means to do them, as long as your wishes are in agreement with my plans."

The first Allobrox said, "We covet nothing more, most worthy Consul, and howsoever we have been tempted lately to a defection and abandonment of allegiance, that does not make us guilty. We are not yet so wretched in our fortunes, nor in our wills so lost, as to abandon a friendship, prodigally, so precious as is the Senate and the people of Rome's, for hopes that do destroy themselves by impetuosity."

"You then are wise, and honest," Cicero said. "Do just this then."

But before telling them what to do, he asked, "When shall you speak with Lentulus and the rest?"

"We are to meet soon, at Brutus' house," the first Allobrox answered.

"Who? Decius Brutus?" Cicero said. "He is not in Rome."

Sanga said, "Oh, but his wife Sempronia —"

Cicero said:

"You, Sanga, inform and remind me: She is a chief figure.

"Well, Allobroges, don't fail to meet them, and to express the best partiality you can pretend to all that they intend. Like it, applaud it, allege that the commonwealth and Senate will be lost to them. Promise them any aids by arms or counsel. What they can desire I would have you anticipate and promise.

"Only, say this: You've had dispatch, in private, by the Consul of your affairs; and, because of the many dangers the state's now in, you are willed by him this evening to depart from Rome, which you by all sought means will do, in order to avoid suspicion."

The words "You've had dispatch" don't say whether the Allobroges' affairs were satisfactorily resolved. The words leave open the possibility that the outcome of the ambassadors' visit to Rome was unsatisfactory.

Cicero continued:

"Now, for the greater authority of the business they've entrusted to you, and to give it credit with your own state at home, say that you desire their letters to your Senate and your people, which once shown you dare pledge both life and honor, and what follows should in every way answer their hopes.

"Those letters being had, offer as an excuse that you have a sudden departure to make. Give me notice at what gate you will go out. I'll have you intercepted and all the letters taken with you, so that you shall be redeemed in all opinions, and they shall be convicted of their manifest treason.

"Evil deeds are well turned back upon their authors; and against an injurer, the revenge is just.

"This must be done now."

"Cheerfully and firmly," the first Allobrox said. "We are men who would rather make haste to undertake it than stay to say so."

"With that assurance and resoluteness, go," Cicero said. "Make yourselves happy while you make Rome so. By means of Sanga, let me have notice and information from you."

“Yes,” the first Allobrox said.

Sempronia and Lentulus talked together.

"When will these creatures, the ambassadors, come?" Sempronia asked. "I would like to see them. Are any of them scholars?"

"I think not, madam," Lentulus said.

"Have they no Greek?" Sempronia asked.

"No, surely," Lentulus answered.

"Bah, what am I doing here, waiting in attendance on them then, if they are nothing but only statesmen?" Sempronia said.

"Yes, your Ladyship shall observe their gravity, their dignity, and their reservedness, their attention to the correctness of their behavior, befitting their positions as ambassadors," Lentulus said.

"I wonder much why states and commonwealths don't employ women to be ambassadors sometimes!" Sempronia said. "We would do as good public service and could make as honorable spies — for so Thucydides calls all ambassadors."

Thucydides wrote *The History of the Peloponnesian War* about a war between Athens and Sparta.

Cethegus entered the scene.

"Have they come, Cethegus?" Sempronia asked.

"Do you ask me?" Cethegus said. "Am I your scout or bawd?"

A scout is a spy; a bawd is a pander. Cethegus did not regard himself as either to Sempronia. One kind of scout is someone who searches for — spies — customers for prostitutes.

"Oh, Caius, it is no such business," Lentulus said.

The business was revolution, not whoring.

Caius Cethegus replied, "No? What does a woman at it, then?"

"Good sir," Sempronia said, "There are those of us women who can be as accomplished traitors as ever a male-conspirator of you all."

"Aye, at smock-treason, matron, I believe you," Cethegus said, "and especially if I were your husband."

Smock-treasure is treason by women. It includes marital infidelity.

Cethegus added, "But when I trust to your cobweb-bosoms any other kind of treason, let me there die a fly and feast you, spider."

Cobwebs snare prey; bosoms can also snare prey.

"You are too sour and harsh, Cethegus," Lentulus said.

"You are kind and courtly," Cethegus replied. "I'd be torn in pieces with wild Hippolytus, nay, I'd undergo the death of every limb, before I'd trust a woman with wind, if I could retain it."

Hippolytus, a son of Theseus, fell from a chariot and was dragged by his horses and torn to pieces.

Cethegus would not entrust a fart to a woman.

"Sir, they'll be trusted with as good secrets yet as you have any, and carry them, too, as close and as concealed as you shall, despite all your courage and resoluteness," Sempronia said.

Cethegus replied, "I'll not contend with you either in speech or behavior, good Calypso."

Calypso was the nymph who held Ulysses as prisoner, preventing him from returning to his wife, Penelope, on his home island of Ithaca.

Longinus entered the scene and said, "The ambassadors have come."

"I give thanks to you, Mercury, who so has rescued me," Cethegus said.

Mercury was the messenger of the gods. He came to Calypso's island with a message from Jupiter ordering her to let Ulysses leave her island.

Gabinius, Statilius, Volturcius, and the Allobroges entered the scene.

"What is the news now, Volturcius?" Lentulus asked.

"They desire some speech with you, in private," Volturcius answered.

"Oh, it is about the prophecy, probably, and the promise of the Sibyl's," Lentulus said.

"It may be," Gabinius said.

Lentulus talked with the Allobroges apart from the others.

"Do they shun me and will not negotiate with me, too?" Sempronia asked.

"No, good lady, you may participate," Gabinius said. "I have told them who you are."

"I should be loath to be left out, and here in my own house, too," Sempronia said.

Cethegus said:

"Can these or such as these be any aids to us? Do they look as if they were built to shake the world, or be of importance to our enterprise? A thousand such as they are could not make one atom — one tiny particle — of our souls.

"They should be men worth heaven's fear, who just by looking up would make Jove stand upon his guard and draw himself inside his thunder which, amazed, he should discharge in vain, and they remain unhurt.

"Or, if they were hurt, then like Capaneus at Thebes they should hang dead upon the highest spires and ask the second bolt to be thrown down."

At Thebes, Capaneus had boasted that not even Jupiter could prevent him from conquering the city. Jupiter was insulted by Capaneus' impiety, and so as Capaneus climbed a ladder to scale the Theban wall, Jupiter killed him with a thunderbolt. Capaneus' corpse, burning, hung from the wall. His limbs burned quickly. According to Statius, author of the epic poem *Thebaid*, if his limbs had burned more slowly, Jupiter would have thrown a second thunderbolt.

Cethegus then said, "Why, Lentulus, do you talk so long? This amount of time would have been enough to have scattered all the stars, to have quenched the sun and moon and made the world despair of day or any light but ours."

Lentulus said to the Allobroges, "How do you like this spirit? In such men Mankind lives. Such souls as these move the world."

"Aye," Sempronia said, "although he finds me hard to bear, I still must do him justice and give him credit. He is a spirit of the right Martian breed."

The Martian spirit is the spirit of Mars, god of war.

The first Allobrox said, "He is a Mars! I wish that we had time to live here and marvel at him."

Lentulus said:

"Well, I see that you would prevent the Consul from coming to an agreement with you. And I commend your care and painstaking attention: It was only reasonable to ask for our letters, and we have prepared them.

"Go in, and we will take an oath and seal them.

"You shall have letters, too, to Catiline. You can visit him on the way back to your country and confirm the alliance.

"This our friend, Volturcius, shall go along with you. Tell our great general that we are ready here; tell him that Lucius Bestia, the Tribune, has been provided with a speech to lay the blame of the war on Cicero; tell him that all long just for his approach and his person. And then you are made freemen like ourselves."

Cicero, Flaccus, and Pomtinius talked together.

Cicero said:

"I cannot doubt the war will succeed well, both because of the honor of the cause and the worth of the man who commands our army. For my colleague and fellow Consul, Antonius, being so ill afflicted with the gout, will not be able to be there in person.

"Therefore, Petreius, his lieutenant, must necessarily take charge of the army. Petreius is much the better soldier, having been a Tribune, Prefect, Lieutenant, and Praetor in the war for thirty years. He is so accustomed to being in the army that he knows all the soldiers by their names."

"They'll fight, then, bravely and splendidly with him," Flaccus said.

"Aye, and he will lead them on as bravely," Pomtinius said.

Cicero said:

"They have a foe who will require them to be brave, whose necessities will arm the foe like a fury.

"But, however, I'll entrust it to the management and the fortune of good Petreius, who's a worthy patriot. Metellus Celer with three legions, too, will stop their course for Gallia."

Two armies were closing in on Catiline's army, ensuring that it could not get reinforcements or escape. Catiline's soldiers could be expected to fight hard simply out of desperation.

Fabius Sanga entered the room.

Cicero asked, "How is the situation now, Fabius?"

"The trick with the Allobrogian ambassadors has worked," Sanga said. "You must immediately place your guards upon the Mulvian Bridge; for by that way they mean to come."

"Then go there, Flaccus and Pomtinius," Cicero said. "I must have you lead that force you have and seize them all. Let not a person escape. The Allobrogian ambassadors will yield and surrender themselves. If there should be any violence, I'll send you aid."

Flaccus and Pomtinius exited.

Cicero then said, "In the meantime, I will call Lentulus to me, as well as Gabinius, and Cethegus, Statilius, Ceparius, and all these by separate messengers. These men no doubt will come without apprehension or suspicion. Prodigal men don't feel their own supplies diminishing. When I have them, I'll place guards upon them so that they will not be able to escape."

"But what'll you do with Sempronia?" Sanga asked.

Cicero replied:

"A state's anger should not take notice either of fools or of women.

"I do not know whether my joy or my sorrow and concern ought to be greater: I have discovered so foul a treason, but also I must undergo the ill-will caused by the doom of so many important men.

"But whatever happens, I will be just. My fortune may forsake me, but not my virtue: That shall go with me, and before me, always, and gladden me, as I do well, although I hear ill things spoken about me."

Flaccus, Pomtinius, and some guards met the loyal Allobroges and the conspirator Volturcius.

"Stand!" Flaccus said. "Who goes there?"

The first Allobrox answered, "We are the Allobroges, and we are friends of Rome."

Pomtinius said, "If you are friends of Rome, then yield yourselves into the custody of the Praetors who, in the name of the whole Senate and the people of Rome, until you clear yourselves, charge you with treachery against the state."

"Die, friends, and don't be taken!" the conspirator Volturcius said.

He fought with the guards.

"What voice is that?" Flaccus said. "Down with them all!"

"We surrender," the Allobroges said.

"Who's he who resists arrest?" Pomtinius said. "Kill him there!"

"Stop! Stop! Stop!" Volturcius said. "I surrender upon conditions."

"We give no conditions to traitors," Flaccus said. "Strike him down! Kill him!"

Volturcius said, "My name is Volturcius; I know Pomtinius."

Pomtinius said, "But he doesn't know you — not while you stand out upon these traitorous terms."

"I'll surrender upon the guarantee of the safety of my life," Volturcius said. "Promise to save my life."

"If it should be forfeited, we cannot save it," Pomtinius said.

"Promise to do your best!" Volturcius said. "I'm not as guilty as many others I can name — and will, if you will grant me leniency."

Pomtinius replied, "All we can do is to deliver you to the Consul."

He meant Cicero.

He then said to the guards, "Take him, and thank the gods who thus have saved Rome."

CHORUS (End of Chapter 4)

The Chorus appeared and criticized the people of Rome:

> *Now do our ears, before our eyes,*
> *Like men in mists [who hear before they see],*
> *Discover who'd [who did] the state surprise [with a sudden attack],*
> *And who resists [opposes such an attack]?*
> *And, as these clouds do yield [give way] to light,*
> *Now do we see*
> *Our thoughts of things, how they did fight*
> *Which seemed t'agree [to agree]?*
> *Of what strange pieces [incompatible components] are we made*
> *Who nothing know*
> *But, as new airs [whispers] our ears invade,*
> *Still censure [judge] so?*
> *That now do hope and now do fear*
> *And now envy,*
> *And then do hate and then love dear,*
> *But know not why;*
> *Or if we do, it is so late*
> *As our best mood [most correct opinion],*
> *Though true, is then thought out of date*
> *And empty of good.*
> *How have we changed and come about*
> *In every doom [person's judgment],*
> *Since wicked Catiline went out*
> *And quitted Rome?*

Having recognized the citizens' changeability and their confusion about events, the Chorus then stated the citizens' changing opinion of Cicero: At first they thought he acted too strongly, and then they thought he had not acted strongly enough:

> *One while [At one time] we thought him [Catiline] innocent,*
> *And then w'accused [we accused]*
> *The Consul for his malice spent [exercised]*

And [his] power abused.
Since that [Because] we [now] hear he [Catiline] is in arms
We think not so,
Yet charge [blame] the Consul with [for] our harms
That [Who] let him go.
[Yet we blame our injuries on the Consul, Cicero, who let Catiline go.]
So in our censure of the state
We still [always] do wander [and fall into error],
And make the careful magistrate
The mark [target] of slander.

The Chorus next recommended that the citizens recognize noble deeds as noble deeds.

What age is this, where honest men
Placed at the helm
A sea of some foul mouth or pen
Shall overwhelm,
And call their diligence deceit,
Their virtue, vice,
Their watchfulness, but lying in wait,
And blood the price [reward they seek]?
Oh, let us pluck this evil seed
Out of our spirits,
And give to every noble deed
The name it merits,
Lest we seem fall'n [fallen], if this endures,
Into those times
To [Where we] love disease and brook [bear] the cures
Worse than the crimes.

CHAPTER 5

— 5.1 —

Petreius and some soldiers stood together at Faesulae, where Catiline and his forces were located. Because of the illness of Antonius, Petreius was now the general of the Senatorial army against Catiline's army. Another army, which was led by Metellus Celer, was keeping Catiline's army from escaping into Transalpine Gaul.

Petreius said:

"It is my fortune and my glory, soldiers, this day to lead you on, the worthy Consul Antonius being kept from the honor of it by disease."

He was referring to the Consul Antonius' being afflicted with the gout.

Petreius continued:

"And I am proud to have so splendid a cause to exercise your arms in. We don't now fight for how long, how broad, how great and large the extent and boundaries of the people of Rome shall be, but to retain what our great ancestors, with all their labors, counsels, arts, and actions, were gaining for us during so many years.

"The quarrel is not now of fame and reputation, of tribute, or of wrongs done to allies, for which and whom the army of the people of Rome was accustomed to move, but for your own republic, for the lofty temples of the immortal gods, for all your fortunes, altars, and your fires and hearths, for the dear souls of your loved wives and children, your parents' tombs, your rites, laws, liberty, and, briefly, for the safety of the world against such men as only by their crimes are known, thrust out by riot, want, or rashness."

The army against the Romans was composed of men who had been thrust out of Rome because of their evil deeds. These men had lived riotously and/or had fallen into poverty and/or were rash and violent.

Petreius then began to describe the enemy forces, which he divided into three sorts:

"One sort, Sulla's old troops, left here in Faesulae, who, suddenly made rich by Sulla's proscriptions in those dire times have since, by their unbounded vast expense, grown needy and poor and have nothing to wait for except new bills and new proscriptions from Catiline."

In history, Catiline had promised his followers new bills, meaning cancellation of debts. The earlier proscriptions of Sulla in history included the murders of many individuals.

However, Petreius' words had another meaning: The new bills would be long-handled weapons of war wielded against the conspirators, and the proscriptions would be of conspirators and would include seizure of their property and lives. The new bills and proscriptions had come into existence because of Catiline.

Petreius continued:

"These men, they say, are valiant; yet I think them not worth your hesitation, if you should hesitate out of fear of them. For either their old virtue has been lost because of their sloth and pleasures, or if their virtue still tarries with them, it is as ill matched to yours as is their small number compared to your number or their unworthy cause compared to your noble cause.

"The second sort are of those who are city-beasts rather than citizens — who, while they reach after our fortunes, have cast away their own. These, whelmed in wine, swelled up with food, and weakened with hourly whoredoms, never left the side of Catiline in Rome, nor are here loosed from his embraces. These men are such as, trust me, never employed their youth in riding or in using well their arms, watching during guard-duty, or doing other military labor. Instead, they just learned to love, drink, dance, and sing, make feasts, and be fine gamesters. And these will wish more hurt to you than they actually bring you."

Petreius then described the final cluster of men he and his soldiers would face:

"The rest are a mixed kind, all sorts of furies, adulterers, dicers, fencers, outlaws, thieves, the murderers of their parents, all the cesspool and plague of Italy met in one torrent to take today from us the punishment due to their evil deeds for so many years."

Petreius then encouraged his soldiers to fight well:

"And who of you, in such a cause and against such fiends, would not now wish himself all arm and weapon to cut such poisons from the earth and let their blood out, to be drawn away in clouds and poured on some uninhabitable place, where the hot sun and slime breeds nothing but monsters?"

The mythical Perseus killed Medusa by decapitating her and then flew on his winged horse over the deserts of Libya. Drops of blood from Medusa's head, which he was carrying, fell onto the desert sands and turned into snakes.

Many people at this time believed that the sun shining on slime resulted in the creation of harmful creatures such as serpents and crocodiles.

Petreius then spoke about the joy in Elysium that awaited any Roman soldiers who died for Rome, and he spoke about the hell that awaited all the enemy soldiers who fought to destroy the Roman Republic:

"Chiefly, when this inevitable joy of our victory shall crown our side, we will know that the least man who falls on our side this day — as some must give their happy names to fate and that eternal memory of the best death recorded with it for their country — shall walk at pleasure in the tents of rest and see far off, beneath him, all the dead enemy soldiers tormented after life, and Catiline there walking, a wretched and less ghost than he, the viewer."

The souls of dead soldiers loyal to Rome would end up in Elysium, where the souls of good men were rewarded. Catiline and his dead soldiers would end up in the part of hell where the souls of bad men were punished.

Petreius continued:

"I'll speak to and urge you on no more; move forward with your eagles and entrust the Senate's and Rome's cause to heaven."

The soldiers said, "To you, to great father Mars, and to greater Jove!"

Both Julius Caesar and Crassus kept a close eye on the politics of Rome. Both would have been happy to take advantage of a successful rebellion against Rome. Both would have been happy after the revolution to push Catiline aside and rule Rome in his place.

"I always expected this from Lentulus, when Catiline was gone," Caesar said.

"I gave them up as lost many days ago," Crassus said.

Caesar asked, "But why did you bear their letter to the Consul that they sent you to give you warning to leave the city so that you would be safe?"

Crassus replied, "Did I know whether he made it? It might come from him for anything I could ascertain for me."

The letter had come from the conspirators and had warned Crassus to leave Rome before a massacre happened. Crassus thought, however, that the letter might have been a forgery commissioned by Cicero to test whether Crassus was loyal to Rome.

Crassus said, "If they meant that I should be safe, among so many to be killed, they might have come, as well as written."

Caesar said, "There is no loss in being secure. I have recently, too, plied him thick with intelligences, but they've been of things he knew before."

By "him," he meant Cicero. The two men were not using names in case they were overheard.

Crassus replied, "A little serves to keep a man upright on these state-bridges, even if the passage were more dangerous."

The state-bridge was like a narrow bridge with Cicero and his allies on one side and with Catiline and his allies on the other side. Until now, Caesar and Crassus had stayed in the middle, not fully committing to either side, but Caesar and Crassus now had to decide which way to cross the bridge. Whose side — Cicero's or Catiline's — would they end up on?

Crassus said, "Let us now take the standing part; let us join the side that will win."

The winning side would stand; the losing side would fall.

Caesar agreed, "We must, and we must be as zealous for it as Cato is. Yet I would like to help these wretched men."

The wretched men were the conspirators in Rome whom Cicero would soon order to be arrested.

"You cannot," Crassus said. "Who would save them who have betrayed themselves?"

Cicero, his brother Quintus, and Cato stood together. Cicero was holding some letters.

"I will not be coerced to do it, brother Quintus," Cicero said. "No man's private enmity and hatred shall make me violate the dignity of another man. If there were proof against Caesar, or whoever, to declare that he is guilty, I would so declare him. But Quintus Catulus and Caius Piso both shall know that the Consul will not for their grudge have any man accused or named falsely."

Quintus Catulus and Caius Piso were two of Julius Caesar's enemies.

Julius Caesar had recently defeated Quintus Catulus in the election for Pontifex Maximus, and he had accused Caius Piso in court of having abused his provincial powers and illegally executing a Gaul.

Cicero's brother, Quintus, replied, "Not falsely, but if any evidence by the Allobroges, or from Volturcius, would sustain the accusation."

"That shall not be sought by me," Cicero said. "If it should reveal itself, I would not spare you, brother, if it pointed at you, trust me."

Cato said, "Good Marcus Tullius — who is more than great — you had your education with the gods."

Marcus Tullius Cicero ordered, "Bring Lentulus here, and arrest the rest of the conspirators in Rome."

He then said to Cato, "This task I am sorry, sir, to give to you."

Caesar, Crassus, Silanus, and other members of the Senate entered the scene.

Cicero said, "I wish what may be always happy and fortunate to Rome and to this Senate."

He showed them the letters he was holding and said, "May it please you, Fathers, to break open the seals of these letters and to view them."

He gave the letters to the Senators, who read them and passed them around.

Cicero then said, "If that which I fear should not be found in them, I yet request of you, at such a time as this, that my diligence and conscientiousness will not be scorned and condemned."

Flaccus and Pomtinius entered the scene.

Cicero asked them, "Have you brought the weapons here from Cethegus' house?"

"They are outside," Flaccus replied.

Cicero ordered, "Be ready with Volturcius, to bring him when the Senate calls, and see that none of the rest confer and talk together."

Flaccus and Pomtinius exited.

Cicero then asked the Senators, "Fathers, what do you read? Is it yet worth your care and concern, if not your fear, what you find written there?"

The letters had been sealed, so Cicero had taken a risk in giving them to the Senators to read. Cicero had believed that the letters were about Catiline's planned rebellion, but he had not been certain that they were.

"It has a face — an appearance — of horror!" Julius Caesar said.

"I am amazed!" Crassus said.

Cato pointed to a letter and said, "Look there."

"Gods!" Silanus said. "Can such men breathe common air?"

Cicero said:

"Although the greatness of the evil, fathers, has often made belief in me small in this Senate, yet since my casting Catiline out of Rome — for now I do not fear the hostility of the words 'cast out' unless the deed be rather to be feared that he went from here alive, when those I meant should follow him did not leave Rome — I have spent both days and nights in watching what the fury and rage of those who stayed in Rome were bent on against my wishes."

He had been carefully watching after the safety of Rome and protecting it against the fury and rage of the conspirators who had stayed in Rome when Catiline left.

Cicero said:

"And I have watched for an opportunity so that I might just take them in that light where, when you perceived their treason with your own eyes, your minds at length would consider your own safety.

"And now it is done. These letters are in their handwriting and sealed with their seals. Their persons, too, are kept in custody, thanks to the gods."

He then ordered, "Bring in Volturcius and the Allobroges."

Flaccus and Pomtinius brought in Volturcius and the Allobroges.

Pointing to the Allobroges, Cicero said, "These are the men who were entrusted with their letters."

"Fathers, believe me, I knew nothing," Volturcius said. "I was travelling to Gallia, and I am sorry —"

Cicero said, "Stop shaking out of fear, Volturcius. Speak the truth and hope — expect — well of this Senate, on the Consul's word."

Cicero was giving his word as Consul that Volturcius could expect mercy from the Senate if he told the truth.

"Since that is the case, I knew everything," Volturcius said. "But truly I was drawn in just the other day."

Julius Caesar said, "Say what you know, and don't be afraid. You have the Senate's faith and the Consul's word to fortify you. The Senate and the Consul will keep their promises."

Volturcius answered, but he was afraid and spoke disjointedly:

"I was sent with letters — and had a message, too — from Lentulus — to Catiline — that he should use all aids — slaves or others — and come with his army as soon to the city as he could — for they were ready and just waited for him — to intercept those who should flee the fire — these men, the Allobroges, did hear it, too."

The first Allobrox said, "Yes, fathers, and they took an oath to us, besides their letters, that we should be free, and they asked us for some immediate aid of horses."

Cicero said, "Here are other testimonies, Fathers: Cethegus' armory."

Cethegus' weapons and armor were brought forth.

"What, not all these?" Crassus said.

Cicero replied, "Here's not the hundredth part of his weapons."

He then ordered, "Call in the fencer, so that we may know the arms that would wield all these weapons."

Calling Cethegus a fencer was an insult. Gladiators were slaves or prisoners of war.

Under guard, Cethegus entered the scene.

Cicero said, "Come, my brave sword-player, to what active use was all this steel provided?"

Cethegus replied, "Had you asked in the days of Sulla, their use would have been to cut throats. But now their use is to look on only. I love to see good blades and feel their edge and points, to put a helmet upon a block and cleave it, and now and then to stab an armor through."

Handing him a letter, Cicero asked, "Do you recognize that letter? That will stab you through. Is it your handwriting?"

Cethegus tore up the letter.

"Stop, save the pieces!" Cicero said.

He then said to Cethegus, "Traitor, has your guilt awakened your fury?"

"I wrote I know not what, nor care not," Cethegus said. "That fool Lentulus dictated the letter and I, the other fool, signed it."

Cicero ordered a guard, "Bring in Statilius: Does he know his handwriting, too? And bring in Lentulus."

Under guard, Statilius and Lentulus entered the scene.

Cicero ordered, "Hand Statilius that letter."

"I confess it all," Statilius said.

Cicero asked Publius Lentulus, "Do you know that seal yet, Publius?"

"Yes, it is mine," Lentulus said.

"Whose image is that on it?" Cicero asked.

"My grandfather's," Lentulus answered.

His grandfather was a patriotic Roman named Publius Cornelius Lentulus; he had been Consul.

"What, that renowned good man, who only embraced his country and loved his fellow citizens!" Cicero said. "Wasn't his picture, although mute, powerful enough to call you away from doing from a deed as foul —"

Lentulus interrupted, "— as what, impetuous Cicero?"

Cicero finished, "— as you are, for I do not know what's fouler."

He pointed to the Allobroges and asked, "Look upon these men. Don't these faces prove your guilt and impudence?"

"What are these men to me?" Lentulus asked. "I don't know them."

"No, Publius?" the first Allobrox said. "We were with you at Brutus' house."

They had met at the house of Decius Brutus, whose wife was Sempronia.

"Last night," Volturcius said.

"What were you doing there?" Lentulus said to the Allobroges. "Who sent for you?"

"You yourself did," the first Allobrox said. "We had letters from you, Cethegus, this Statilius here, Gabinius Cimber, all but from Longinus, who would not write because he was to come shortly in person after us, he said, to take charge of the horses that we should levy."

"And he has fled to Catiline, I hear," Cicero said.

"Spies? Spies?" Lentulus said.

He was referring to the Allobroges.

The Allobroges said to Lentulus, "You told us, too, about the Sibyl's books, and how you were to be a king this year, the twentieth from the burning of the Capitol. You told us that three Cornelii were to reign in Rome, of which you were the last; and you praised Cethegus and the great spirits who were with you in the action."

Cethegus said to Lentulus, sarcastically, "These are your honorable ambassadors, my sovereign lord."

Cato said, "Shut up, too bold Cethegus!"

The first Allobrox said, "Besides Gabinius and your agent — Umbrenus — you named Autronius, Servius Sulla, Vargunteius, and some others."

Volturcius said to Lentulus:

"I had letters from you to Catiline, and a message that I've told to the Senate, truly, word for word; for which I hope they will be gracious to me.

"I was drawn in by that same wicked Cimber, and I thought there would be no hurt at all."

Cimber was Gabinius. "Cimber" was an epithet meaning "cruel." He was Gabinius Cimber: Gabinius the Cruel.

Cicero said:

"Volturcius, peace. Be silent.

"Where is your visor — your mask, your pretense of innocence — or your voice now, Lentulus? Are you confounded? Why don't you answer that question? Is all so clear, so plain, so manifest that both your eloquence and your impudence, and your ill nature, too, have left you at once?"

Cicero then ordered the guards, "Take him aside. There's yet one more: Gabinius, the engineer — the plotter — of all."

Under guard, Gabinius entered the scene.

Cicero ordered, "Show him that letter. Let's see if he recognizes it."

"I know nothing," Gabinius said.

"No?" Cicero asked.

"No," Gabinius answered. "Neither will I know."

Cato said, "Impudent head! Impudent disposition! Stick his words back into his throat. If I were the Consul, I'd make you eat the evil you have vented."

"Is there a law for it, Cato?" Gabinius asked.

"Do you ask about a law, you who would have broken all the laws of nature, manhood, conscience, and religion?" Cato replied.

"Yes, I may ask for it," Gabinius Cimber said.

"No, pernicious Cimber," Cato said. "The inquiring after good does not belong to a wicked person."

"Aye, but Cato does nothing except by law," Gabinius said.

Cato had a reputation for righteousness.

Crassus said to the guards, "Take Gabinius aside. There's proof enough, although he doesn't confess."

"Wait, I will confess," Gabinius said. "All's true your spies have told you. Make much of them. Praise them well."

Cethegus said, "Yes, and reward them well, for fear you get no more such. See that they do not die in a ditch and stink, now you have finished with them, or beg on the bridges here in Rome, whose arches their active industry and toil have saved."

Many beggars begged on the bridges of Rome. It's harder to avoid beggars on a bridge than beggars in a street.

Cicero said:

"See, fathers, what minds and spirits these are who, being convicted of such a treason and by such a multitude of witnesses, dare still retain their boldness. What would their rage have done if they had conquered?

"I thought, when I had thrust out Catiline, neither the state nor I should need to have feared Lentulus' lethargic sleep here, nor Longinus' fat, nor this Cethegus' rashness. It was only Catiline I watched while he was within our walls, as the one who had the brain, the hand, the heart.

"But now we find the contrary! Where was there a people grieved, or a state discontent, able to make or help a war against Rome, but these, the Allobroges? And the conspirators found those men: the Allobroges.

"If the just gods had not been pleased to make the Allobroges friends to our safety more than to their own, as it then seemed, neglecting and despising these traitorous men's offers, where would we have been, or where would the commonwealth have been, when their great chief — Catiline — had been called home to Rome?"

Lentulus' letter, which the Allobroges had turned over to Cicero, called for Catiline to return to Rome.

Cicero pointed to Lentulus and said:

"This man, their absolute king — whose noble grandfather, armed in pursuit of the seditious Caius Gracchus, took a brave wound for dear defense of that which Lentulus would spoil — had gathered all his aids of ruffians, slaves, and other slaughtermen, and he had given us — the Senators — up for murder to Cethegus.

"The other rank of citizens — the non-Senators — he gave up to Gabinius, the city was to be set on fire by Cassius, and Italy, nay, the world, was to be laid waste by cursed Catiline and his accomplices.

"Imagine it, Fathers, just think that with me you saw this glorious city, the light of all the earth, the tower of all nations, suddenly falling in one flame.

"Imagine you viewed your country buried under the heaps of slaughtered citizens who had no grave.

"Imagine this Lentulus here reigning, as he dreamt he would do, and imagine those conspirators his purple Senate."

This society called the color of blood purple, and Roman Senators wore a tunic or a toga with a purple stripe.

Cicero continued:

"Imagine Catiline come with his fierce army; and imagine the cries of matrons, the flight of children, and the rape of virgins.

"Imagine the shrieks of the living, with the dying groans on every side to assault your sense of hearing.

"Imagine these things happening until the blood of Rome becomes mixed with her ashes!

"This was the spectacle these fiends intended to please their malice."

Cethegus said, "Aye, and it would have been a brave one, Consul. But your part would then not have been as long as now it is. I would have quite spoiled and defeated your oration and slit that fine rhetorical pipe of yours in the first scene."

"Insolent monster!" Cato said.

Cicero asked, "Fathers, is it your pleasures they shall be committed to some safe but free custody, until the Senate makes some other decision?"

A safe but free custody would be in a private home rather than in a prison. A leading citizen would be responsible for the detained person.

"It pleases us well," the Senators said.

Cicero said:

"Then, Marcus Crassus, you take charge of Gabinius; send him home to your house.

"You, Caesar, take charge of Statilius.

"Cethegus shall be sent to Cornificius, and Lentulus shall be sent to Publius Lentulus Spinther, who now is an Aedile."

Cato said, "It would be best for the Praetors to convey them under guard to their respective houses and hand them over."

"Let it be so," Cicero said.

He then ordered the Praetors, "Take them away from here."

Julius Caesar said, "But first let Lentulus divest himself of his Praetorship."

"I resign my Praetorship here to the Senate," Lentulus said.

He removed his robe that indicated his rank.

Officials such as Praetors could not be imprisoned while in office.

"So, now there's no offence done to religion," Julius Caesar said.

Praetors could take the auspices, the performance of which was a religious rite. Julius Caesar had been elected Pontifex Maximus — the chief priest of the official state religion — and so he was concerned about offence done to religion. Now that Lentulus was no longer a Praetor, he could be imprisoned without offense done to religion.

"Caesar, it was piously and timely urged," Cato said.

Flaccus, Pomtinius, and some guards exited with Lentulus, Cethegus, Statilius, and Gabinius.

Cicero asked the Senators, "What do you decree to the Allobroges who threw light on and revealed this rebellion by providing information?"

"A free grant from the state of all their suits," Crassus said.

"And a reward out of the public treasury," Julius Caesar said.

"Aye, and the title of honest men to crown them," Cato said.

"What about Volturcius?" Cicero asked.

Once captured, Volturcius had informed on the other conspirators in return for mercy.

"Life and mercy are a good reward enough for him," Julius Caesar said.

"I ask no more," Volturcius said.

"Yes, yes, some money," Cato said. "You need it. It will keep you honest: Poverty made you a knave."

Silanus said, "Let Flaccus and Pomtinius, the Praetors, have public thanks, and Quintus Fabius Sanga, too, for their good service."

"They all deserve it," Crassus said.

Cato asked, "But what do we decree to the Consul — Cicero — whose virtue, counsel, watchfulness, and wisdom have freed the commonwealth and, without tumult, slaughter, or blood, or scarcely raising an army, rescued us all out of the jaws of fate?"

"We owe our lives to him, and our fortunes," Crassus said.

"Our wives, our children, our parents, and our gods," Julius Caesar said.

"We all are saved by his fortitude and moral courage," Silvanus said.

"The commonwealth owes him a civic garland," Cato said. "He is the only father of his country."

A *corona civica*, or civic garland, which was made of oak leaves, was a reward for saving the lives of citizens. Another great honor was being given the title *pater patriae*: father of his country.

"Let there be public prayer to all the gods made in that name for him," Julius Caesar said.

Crassus said:

"And in these words:

"*Because he has by his vigilance preserved Rome from the flame, the Senate from the sword, and all her citizens from massacre.*"

Cicero said, "How my labors are more than paid, grave Fathers, in these great titles and decreed honors!"

Cicero was the first Roman to be given these honors because of his devotion to his civic duty rather than for military victories. He had deserved these titles and honors not because he had acted as a general on a battlefield, but because he had acted as a statesman in Rome.

Cicero said:

"Ever since Rome became Rome, I am the first of the civil robe to receive these titles and honors, and I have received them from this frequent — full, well-attended — Senate, which more gladdens me because I now see you have the sense of your own safety.

"If those good days come no less pleasing to us wherein we are preserved from some great danger than those wherein we're born and brought to light — because the gladness of our safety is certain, but the condition of our birth not so, and because we are saved with pleasure, but are born without the sense of joy —"

We take pleasure in being saved as adults because we are aware that we are being saved, but an infant who is being born does not have the knowledge needed to feel pleasure at being born. An infant does not know the condition of his or her birth — is the infant born into the Senatorial class or is the infant born into a family that cannot feed it?

If we are saved, we know that we have been saved and we feel pleased that we have been saved. Being born is most likely a scary process for the infant. Most infants cry immediately after birth.

When Rome was born — founded — no one could know (outside of mythology) how great it would become.

Cicero's listeners knew how great a city (and empire) had been saved through Cicero's efforts.

Cicero continued, "— why shouldn't then this day, to us and all descendants of ours, be had in equal fame and honor with that when Romulus first reared these walls, when so much more is saved than he built?"

The founding of Rome was an important event, and the saving of Rome — and all that Rome had acquired and accomplished since its founding — was an important event.

"It ought to be," Julius Caesar said.

"Let it be added to our *fasti* — calendar — as an important historical event," Crassus said.

Loud voices sounded outside.

"What tumult's that?" Cicero asked.

Flaccus entered the scene and said, "Here's one Tarquinius captured, going to Catiline, and he says he was sent by Marcus Crassus, whom he names as one guilty of the conspiracy."

"He is some lying varlet," Cicero said. "Take him away to prison."

"Bring him in and let me see him," Marcus Crassus requested.

"He is not worth it, Crassus," Cicero said.

He then ordered, "Keep Tarquinius shut up in prison, and hungry, until he tells by whose pernicious counsel he dares to slander so great and good a citizen as Crassus."

Crassus said to himself, "By yours, I fear it will turn out."

Crassus suspected that Cicero himself was the source of the pernicious counsel that had led to the slander or "slander" against him.

Silanus said to Crassus, "Some of the traitors, to be sure, in order to give their action the more credibility, told him to name you, or any man."

Cicero said, "I myself know, by all the course of events of this business, that Crassus is noble and just, and he loves his country."

Flaccus said, "Here is a document, too, accusing Caesar, from Lucius Vectius and confirmed by Curius."

"Away with all of that," Cicero said. "Throw it out of the court."

"A trick on me, too?" Julius Caesar said.

"It is some men's malice," Cicero said. "I said to Curius that I did not believe him."

"Wasn't that Curius your spy who had a reward decreed to him in the last meeting of the Senate along with Fulvia, upon your private motion?" Caesar asked.

Cicero had specifically requested a reward for Curius and for Fulvia.

"Yes," Cicero said.

"But he has not received that reward yet?" Julius Caesar asked.

"No," Cicero said. "Don't let this trouble you, Caesar; no one believes his accusation."

"It shall not, as long as he receives no reward," Julius Caesar said. "But if he does receive a reward, surely I shall think my reputation for loyalty to be very uncertain and unsafe, where such as he is may receive pay to accuse me."

"You shall have no wrong done to you, noble Caesar," Cicero said. "Instead, you shall have all satisfaction and contentment."

"Consul, I am silent," Julius Caesar said.

He was satisfied and content with Cicero's statement.

Catiline addressed his soldiers in his military camp:

"I never yet knew, soldiers, that words added virtue to valiant men in a battle, or that a general's oration made an army fall or stand; but how much military prowess and valor, formed by habit or inherent in his nature, each man's breast was owner of, so much in action it showed.

"It is in vain to seek to influence with speech a man whom neither glory nor danger can excite; for the mind's fear keeps all brave sounds from entering at that ear.

"Yet I would remind you of some few things, my friends, and give you reasons for my present plans and course of action.

"You know no less than I what state, what point and conditions, our affairs stand in. And you all have heard what a calamitous misery the sloth and sluggishness of Lentulus has plucked both on himself and on us.

"And you all have heard how, while our aids there in the city looked for are defeated, our entrance into Gallia, too, is stopped. Two armies lie in wait for us: one from Rome, the other from the provinces in Gaul. And where we are, although I most desire it, our great need of grain and other foods forbids us to stay longer. So necessarily we must move away from here, but the sword must both point to and cut the passage to where we move.

"I therefore wish you, when you strike, only to have your courage and your souls about you, and think you carry in your laboring hands the things you seek, glory and liberty, your country that you want now, with the fates that are to be instructed by our swords."

Usually, ancient people believed that fate is fixed and actions are what is fated. Catiline, however, was saying that his soldiers' swords would determine their fate.

Catiline continued:

"If we can give the conquering blow, all will be safe and secure for us. We shall not lack provisions, nor supplies. The colonies and free towns will lie open to us.

"Whereas, if we yield to fear, expect no place nor friend to shelter those whom their own fortune and ill-used arms have left without protection.

"You might have lived in servitude, or exile, or safe at Rome, depending on the politically powerful great ones except that you thought those things unfit for men.

"And in that thought you then were valiant. For no man ever yet exchanged peace for war except he who meant to conquer. Hold that purpose. Keep that intention. There's more necessity you should be conquerors who are fighting for yourselves than those men who are fighting for others.

"That man is base who trusts his feet although his hands are armed — a noble man will not flee while he holds a weapon in his arms.

"I think I see Death and the Furies waiting to see what we will do, and all the gods in heaven at leisure to watch the great spectacle. Draw then your swords, and if our destiny envies our courage and begrudges it the honor of the day, let us still take care to sell ourselves at such a price as may destroy the world to buy us, and to make Fate, while she attacks ours, fear her own estate."

Pomtinius, Cicero, Silanus, Cato, Caesar, Crassus, and other members of the Senate stood together, along with some Lictors. They were going to decide the punishment of the conspirators who had been captured in Rome — without a trial.

"What is the meaning of this hasty calling of the Senate?" the first Senator said.

"We shall know immediately," the second Senator said. "Wait until the Consul speaks."

Pomtinius said:

"Fathers conscript, think about your safeties and what to do with these conspirators. Some of their clients, their freedmen — slaves they had freed — and their slaves begin to raise troops and start an insurrection."

There had been attempts to rescue the conspirators.

Pomtinius continued:

"One of Lentulus' bawds runs up and down the shops, through every street, with money to corrupt the poor artisans and needy tradesmen to their aid.

"Cethegus has sent, too, to his servants, who are many, picked out especially, and trained in bold assaults, to tell them that forthwith they should arm themselves and attempt to rescue him.

"All will be in instant uproar, if you don't prevent it with immediate plans. We have done what we can to meet the fury, and we will do more."

Guards had been stationed throughout Rome.

Pomtinius concluded:

"Be good to yourselves."

Cicero addressed the Senators:

"What is your pleasure, Fathers, that shall be done?

"Silanus, you are the Consul-elect; you will be the next Consul. What is your recommendation of the sentence to give these men?"

The Roman custom was for the Consul-elect to give his judicial opinion first. Once he took office, the Consul-elect would likely deal with much of the aftermath of the carrying out of the Senate's sentence.

It was also the Roman custom, however, not to execute Roman citizens without giving them a trial. Lentulus and the other captured conspirators had not been given trials.

Silanus said:

"My recommendation is short, and it is this:

"Since the conspirators have sought to blot the name of Rome out of the world and raze this glorious empire with her own hands and arms turned on herself, I think it fitting that they die.

"And if my breath could now execute them, they should not enjoy a moment of time or tinge of light longer, to poison this our common air."

"I think so, too," the first Senator said.

"And I," the second Senator said.

"And I," the third Senator said.

"And I," the fourth Senator said.

Cicero asked, "What is the sentence you recommend, Caius Caesar?"

Caius Julius Caesar said:

"Conscript Fathers, in great affairs, and in uncertain and controversial affairs, it behooves men who are asked their sentence to be free from either hate or love, anger or pity. For where the least of these hinders, there the mind does not easily discern the truth.

"I speak this to you in the name of Rome, for whom you stand, and to the case before us now:

"I say that this foul crime of Lentulus and the rest should not more prevail with you than your dignity, and you should not be more indulgent to your feelings than to your honor.

"If there could be found a pain or punishment equal to their crimes, I would help devise a plan for it and help execute it.

"But if the greatness of what they have done exceeds all man's invention, I think it fitting to stop where our laws do.

"Poor petty states may alter their policies at their whim. And if they offend with anger, few know it because they are obscure; their fame and fortune are equal and the same — they are small.

"But the states that are the head of the world and live in that seen height, all mankind knows their actions.

"So we see the greater fortune has the lesser license and freedom of action. They must neither favor nor hate, nor be the least angry, for what with others is called anger, there is cruelty and pride.

"I know Silanus, who spoke before me, is a just, valiant man, a lover of the state, and one who would not in such a business use either judicial grace or judicial hatred.

"I also know well his manners and his modesty. Nor do I think his sentence cruel — for against such delinquents, what can be too bloody?

"But it is true that sentence is unacceptable to our state, since to an offending citizen of Rome our laws prescribe exile, and not death.

"Why then decrees he that? It would be wrong to think he decrees that out of fear, when, by the diligence of so worthy a Consul, all is made safe and secure.

"Is it for punishment? Why, death's the end of evils, and a rest rather than a torment. It dissolves all griefs, and beyond death is neither worry nor joy.

"You hear that my recommended sentence would not have them die.

"What is my recommended sentence then?

"Set them free and increase Catiline's army? So will they, if they are just banished.

"No, grave fathers, I would sentence them, first, to have their estates confiscated, and then, to have their persons remain prisoners in the free towns, far off from Rome and severed from it and from each other, where they might have relation hereafter neither to the Senate nor to the people.

"Or if they should have, those towns that were guarding them then would be fined as enemies to the state."

The first Senator said, "What Caesar has uttered is good and honorable."

Cicero said:

"Fathers, I see your faces and your eyes are all turned toward me, to see which of these two censures I prefer. Both censures are grave and corresponding to the dignity of the speakers and the greatness of the affair, and both censures are severe.

"One — Silanus — urges death; and he may well remember that this state has punished wicked citizens so.

"The other — Caesar — urges restraints, and those perpetual, which he thinks are devised as more appropriate punishments.

"Decree which you shall please. You have a Consul who is not readier to obey than to defend whatever you shall enact for the republic, and meet with willing shoulders any burden, or any fortune with equanimity, though it were death, which to a valiant man can never happen foul, nor to a Consul be premature, or to a wise man be wretched."

Valiant men, Consuls, and wise men are always ready for death.

Consul-elect Silanus said, "Fathers, I spoke only as I thought the needs of the commonwealth required."

Cato said, "Don't excuse your recommendation."

Cicero said, "Cato, speak your recommended sentence."

Cato said:

"This it is.

"You here dispute about kinds of punishment and stand consulting about what you should decree against those whom you rather should beware.

"This evil deed is not like those common crimes that, when they are done, the laws may prosecute.

"But this evil deed, if you don't prevent it before it happens, will not wait for your judgment once it has happened."

The evil deed was revolution. Although these conspirators had been arrested, Catiline had an army and remained a danger to Rome.

If they could, most or all of the conspirators would join Catiline.

Cato continued:

"Good Caius Caesar here has very well and subtly discoursed of life and death, as if he thought those things a pretty fable that are related to us of Hell and Furies, or of the diverse way that evil men go from good to filthy, dark, and ugly places.

"And therefore he would have these live, and live long, too, but far from Rome and in the small free towns, lest here they might have rescue — as if men fit for such acts were only in the city, and not throughout all Italy! Or that boldness could not do more where it found least resistance!

"It is foolish advice, if he thinks the conspirators we have in custody are dangerous.

"And if he does not consider the conspirators dangerous, and he alone amid the so great fear of all men stands not frightened, he gives me cause, and you, more to fear him."

If Julius Caesar alone was not frightened, then it could be because he himself was a secret conspirator.

Cato continued:

"I speak plainly, Fathers.

"Here you look about, one at another, doubting what to do, with faces as if you trusted to the gods who always have saved you — and they can do it.

"But neither wishings nor base womanish prayers can draw their aids, but only vigilance, counsel, action, which they will be ashamed to forsake.

"It is sloth the gods hate, and cowardice.

"Here you have the traitors in your houses, yet you stand doubting what to do with them. Let them loose, and send them away from here with arms, too, with the result that your mercy may become your misery as soon as it can.

"Some may say, 'Oh, but they are great men, and they have offended only through ambition. We would spare their honor.'

"Aye, if they themselves had spared it, or their reputation, or their modesty, or either god or man, then I would spare them.

"But, as things now stand, Fathers, to spare these men would be to commit a greater wickedness than that which you would revenge.

"If there would be time and place for you to correct this error of sparing these conspirators' lives, you should make it. It would be your punishment to feel your error of being dilatory and slow to do what needs to be done.

"But there is not time and place. Instead, necessity now bids me say to you: Let them not live an hour, if you intend that Rome should live a day.

"I have finished."

"Cato has spoken like an oracle," the first Senator said.

"Let it be so decreed," Crassus said.

"We are all fearful," the second Senator said.

"And we would have been base, had not Cato's virtue raised us," Silanus said.

"Proceed, most worthy Consul," the third Senator said. "We'll assist you."

"I'm not yet changed in my opinion about the sentence, Fathers," Julius Caesar said.

"That doesn't matter," Cato said.

A servant carrying letters entered the scene.

Cato asked the servant, "What are those?"

The servant replied, "Letters for Caesar."

He handed the letters to Caesar and then exited.

"From whom?" Cato asked. "Let them be read in the open Senate. Fathers, they come from the conspirators. I crave to have them read, for the benefit of the republic."

Julius Caesar said, "Cato, you read it."

He handed a letter to Cato and said quietly to him, "It is a love letter from your dear sister to me. Although you hate me, do not make the letter public."

Cato's half-sister was Servilia. She was the mother of Brutus, a future assassin of Julius Caesar, with whom she was having an affair. She was also the wife of Consul-elect Silanus.

Believing Caesar and unwilling to make the contents of the letter public, Cato returned the letter and said, "Keep the letter, drunkard."

He could have called Caesar an adulterer, but that would have meant calling his half-sister an adulterer, too.

Cato said to Cicero, "Consul, go forth, confidently."

Julius Caesar said, "You'll repent this rashness, Cicero."

In fact, Cicero would suffer consequences for the executions of Roman citizens without first giving them a trial. Cicero would be prosecuted four years later for the execution of Lentulus, although Lentulus' sentence of death was awarded by the Senate. As a result, Cicero went into voluntary exile.

Drawing his sword, Pomtinius said, "Caesar shall repent it."

"Stop, friends!" Cicero ordered.

"Caesar is scarcely a friend to the people of Rome," Pomtinius said.

"No violence!" Cicero said. "Caesar, you are safe."

Cicero then ordered the Lictors, "Lead on."

The Lictors carried out the sentences the Senate gave to offenders. They would escort Cicero to the places where the conspirators were being held.

Cicero asked, "Where are the public executioners?"

He then said to Pomtinius, "Tell them to come to us."

Pomtinius exited.

Cicero then said to the Lictors, "Let's go to Spinther's house."

Publius Lentulus Spinther was responsible for guarding the conspirator Publius Cornelius Lentulus.

They went there, and Cicero said, "Bring Lentulus forth."

Pomtinius returned with the public executioners.

Lentulus arrived, under guard.

Cicero said to the executioners, "Here, you, the grave revengers of capital crimes against the public, take this man to your justice. Strangle him."

Lentulus said to Cicero, "You do well, Consul. It was a cast at dice — a matter of chance — in Fortune's hand, not long since, that you yourself would have heard these or other words as fatal."

In other words, if things had turned out differently, it would be you, Cicero, who would die.

The executioners exited with Lentulus in their custody.

Cicero said to the Lictors, "Lead us on to Quintus Cornificius' house."

They went there, and Cicero said, "Bring forth Cethegus."

Cethegus, under guard, entered the scene.

The public executioners returned.

Cicero said to the public executioners, "Take him to the appropriate death that he has deserved, and let it be said: 'He was once.'"

"He was once" meant "he once existed and now he does not," but Cethegus treated it as an incomplete sentence that he now completed.

He said, "— a beast or, what is worse, a slave, Cethegus. Let that be the name for all that's base hereafter: that Cethegus would let this worm Cicero pronounce on him, Cethegus, and not have trampled Cicero's body into — Ha! Aren't you angered?"

Cicero replied, "Justice is never angry."

He then said to the executioners, "Take him away."

Cethegus said, "Oh, the whore Fortune and her bawds, the Fates, who put these tricks on men who knew the way to death by a sword! Strangle me, so I may sleep; I shall grow angry with the gods else."

Death by strangulation was regarded as a base death; death by a sword was much to be preferred.

Cethegus wanted to sleep after death. If the gods were to put his ghost in the Land of the Dead, he would be angry at them.

The executioners exited with Cethegus under guard.

Cicero said to the Lictors, "Lead us to Caius Caesar's, for Statilius."

They went there, and Cicero said, "Bring him and savage Gabinius out."

Gabinius and Statilius, under guard, entered the scene.

The public executioners returned.

Cicero said to the executioners, "Here, take them into your cold hands and let them feel death from you."

"I thank you," Gabinius said. "You do me a pleasure."

"And me, too," Statilius said.

The executioners exited with Gabinius and Statilius under guard.

Cato said to Marcus Tullius Cicero:

"So, Marcus Tullius, you may now stand up and call Rome happy because you are its Consul.

"Great parent of your country, go and let the old men of the city, before they die, kiss you. Let the matrons hang about your neck. Let the youths and maidens store up in their memory in preparation for when they are old what kind of man you were, so they can tell their nephews about you when, some year in the future, they read within our *fasti* about your Consulship."

Petreius entered the scene.

"Who's this?" Cato asked. "Petreius?"

"Welcome," Cicero said. "Welcome, renowned soldier. What's the news? This face can bring no ill with it to Rome. How is the worthy Consul, my colleague Antonius?"

"As well as victory can make him, sir," Petreius said. "He greets the fathers, and to me he has entrusted the sad relation of the civil strife, for in such civil war, even victory is still black."

"Shall we withdraw into the Temple of Concord?" Cicero asked.

"No, happy, fortunate Consul," Cato said. "Let's stay here; let all ears take the benefit of this tale. If he — Petreius — had a loud enough voice to extend to the poles and strike it through the center to the antipodes on the other side of the world, the tale would ask for it."

Petreius said:

"The straits and needs of Catiline being such that he must fight with one of the two armies that then had nearly enclosed and surrounded him, it pleased Fate to make us the object of his desperate choice, wherein the danger almost peised — counterbalanced — the honor.

"As Catiline rose and took up arms, the day grew black because of him, and Fate descended nearer to the earth, as if she meant to hide the name of things under her wings and make the world her quarry.

"At this we roused, lest one small minute's delay would have left it to be inquired what Rome was. And, as we ought, armed in confidence of our great cause, we in battle formation stood.

"Catiline advanced, not with the face of any man, but with the face of a public ruin. His countenance was a civil war itself. And all his soldiers had showing in their faces the paleness of the death that was to come.

"Yet they cried out like vultures and urged each other on, as if they would precipitate our fates, nor did we stay longer for them. We immediately advanced toward them.

"But Catiline himself struck the first stroke; and with it fled a life, which being cut, it seemed as if a narrow neck of land had broken between two mighty seas, and each flowed into the other, for so did the slaughter, and whirled about, as when two violent tides meet and do not yield.

"The Furies stood on hills circling the place and trembled to see men do more than they. Meanwhile, Piety left the field, grieved for that side that in so bad a cause they didn't know what a crime their valor was.

"The Sun-chariot stood still and was, behind the cloud the battle made, seen sweating and laboring to drive up its frightened horses whom still the noise drove backward.

"And now fierce Enyo, like a flame, would have consumed all it could reach, and then itself, had not the fortune of the commonwealth come Pallas-like to every Roman thought."

Enyo is the goddess of war. In this passage, she is metaphorically war.

Pallas is Pallas Athena, goddess of wisdom. The loyal Roman army wisely remembered Rome and so fought fiercely. What was consumed was not both armies but only Catiline's army.

Another Pallas is the son of King Evander, who lived in Italy. This young Pallas fought on the side of Aeneas, a survivor of the Trojan War who became an important ancestor of the Roman people, in Virgil's *Aeneid*. Pallas died in the fighting, but Aeneas won the war.

Petreius continued:

"Catiline seeing that, and also seeing that now his troops covered that earth they'd fought on with their dead trunks, he, ambitious for great fame, to crown his evil, collected all his fury and ran, armed with a glory high as his despair, into our army, like a Libyan lion running upon his hunters, scornful of our weapons, not caring about wounds, plucking down lives about him, until he had circled in himself with death, surrounded by our soldiers.

"Then fell he, too, to embrace it — death — where it lay. And as in that rebellion against the gods, Minerva extending in her hands Medusa's head (seeing which turns men into stone), one of the giant brethren — Enceladus — felt himself turn into marble at the fatal sight and, now almost made stone, began to inquire what flint, what rock it was that crept through all his limbs, and, before he could think more, he had become that which he feared he would become, so Catiline, at the sight of Rome in us, became his tomb; yet did his look retain some of his fierceness, and his hands still moved, as if he labored yet to grasp the state with those rebellious parts of his body."

Cato said, "His was a brave, bad death. Had this death been loyal, now, and as for his country as it was against it, who previously had fallen greater than he?"

Cicero said, "Honored Petreius, Rome, not I, must thank you."

He then said about Petreius, "How modestly has he spoken of himself!"

"He did the more," Cato agreed.

Petreius had been the general of the Roman army. He was largely responsible for its success in battle.

Cicero said:

"Thanks to the immortal gods, Romans, I now am paid for all my labors, my watchings, and my dangers. Here conclude your praises, triumphs, honors, and rewards decreed to me.

"Only the memory of this glad day, if I may know it shall live within your thoughts, shall much affect and influence my conscience, which I must always prefer before fame.

"Though both be good, the latter yet is worst,

"And always is ill gotten without the first."

NOTES
— 4.2 —

Remember who I am, and of what place,
What petty fellow this is that opposes:
One that hath exercised his eloquence 100
Still to the bane of the nobility,
A boasting, insolent tongue-man.
(4.2.98-102)
Source of Above:
The Cambridge Edition of the Works of Ben Jonson
7 Volume Set. Volume 4.
Ben Jonson (Author), David Bevington (Editor), Martin Butler (Editor), Ian Donaldson (Editor).
Cambridge University Press, 2012. Print. P. 127.
The below information comes from an article titled "SOCIAL CLASS AND PUBLIC DISPLAY":

Upper Classes

Senatorial class (*senatores*): The basis for this class was **political**. It included all men who served in the Senate, and by extension their families. This class was dominated by the **nobles** (*nobiles*), families whose ancestors included at least one Consul (earlier the qualification had been a curule magistracy, i.e. curule aedile and up). The first man in his family to be elected Consul, thus qualifying his family for noble status, was called a "new man" (*novus homo*), although this term was used in varying senses—it could refer to an equesterian [sic] who was the first in his family to be elected to political office and thus join the senatorial class, or to a man from the senatorial class who was the first in his family to be elected Consul and thus join the nobles, or most dramatically to an equestrian like Cicero who was elected Consul. Senators had to prove that they had property worth at least 1,000,000 sesterces; there was no salary attached to service in the Senate, and senators were prohibited from engaging personally in nonagricultural business, trade or public contracts. Men of the senatorial class wore the tunic with broad stripes (*laticlavi*).

Equestrian class (*equites*): The basis for this class was **economic**. A man could be formally enrolled in the equestrian order if he could prove that he possessed a stable minimum amount of wealth (property worth at least 400,000 sesterces); by extension his family members were also considered equestrians. However, if an equestrian was elected to a magistracy and entered the Senate, he moved up to the senatorial class; this was not particularly easy or frequent. Equestrians were primarily involved in the types of business prohibited to senators. Equestrians wore the tunic with narrow stripes (*angusti clavi*).

Source of Above:
"SOCIAL CLASS AND PUBLIC DISPLAY
Barbara F. McManus[1]
The College of New Rochelle
bmcmanus@cnr.edu
January, 2009

***

The below information comes from the Wikipedia article titled "Cicero":

Cicero's cognomen, or personal surname, comes from the Latin for chickpea[2], cicer. Plutarch explains that the name was originally given to one of Cicero's ancestors who had a cleft in the tip of his nose resembling a chickpea. However, it is more likely that Cicero's ancestors prospered through the cultivation and sale of chickpeas. Romans often chose down-to-earth personal surnames. The famous family names of Fabius, Lentulus, and Piso come from the Latin names of beans, lentils,

---

1.   http://www.cnr.edu/home/bmcmanus/

2. *https://en.wikipedia.org/wiki/Chickpea*

*and peas, respectively. Plutarch writes that Cicero was urged to change
this deprecatory name when he entered politics, but refused, saying that
he would make Cicero more glorious than Scaurus[3] ("Swollen-ankled")
and Catulus[4] ("Puppy").*

Source: "Cicero." Wikipedia. Accessed 13 July 2021
< https://en.wikipedia.org/wiki/Cicero >.

---

3. *https://en.wikipedia.org/wiki/Marcus_Aemilius_Scaurus_(consul_115_BC)*

4. *https://en.wikipedia.org/wiki/Gaius_Lutatius_Catulus*

— 4.2 —

Was on the fifth, the Kalends of November,
(4.2.187)
Source of Above:
The Cambridge Edition of the Works of Ben Jonson
7 Volume Set. Volume 4.
Ben Jonson (Author), David Bevington (Editor), Martin Butler (Editor), Ian Donaldson (Editor).
Cambridge University Press, 2012. Print. P. 127.
According to *The Cambridge Edition of the Works of Ben Jonson*, this is October 28.

***

The Kalends is the first of the month, and days were counted before the Kalends. The Kalends itself is one of the days counted; in other words, the counting is inclusive.

> *Ante diem quintum Kalendas Novembres*
> October 28: fifth day before Kalends
> October 29: fourth day before Kalends
> October 30: third day before Kalends
> October 31: day before Kalends
> November 1: Kalends of November

Source of Above:
http://www.medievalgenealogy.org.uk/cal/novsas.htm
The three-month calendar depicted on the web page below agrees with October 28 as the correct date:
http://www.medievalgenealogy.org.uk/cal/novsas.htm
For More Information: "A Medieval English Calendar"
http://www.medievalgenealogy.org.uk/cal/medcal.shtml
The below is a note from Lynn Harold Harris' edition of *Catiline*:

Was, on the fifth (the Kalends of Nouember).

W.'s emendation is undoubtedly right, and the line should read: on the fifth o' the Kalends of November. *Q2 omits the parenthesis, but lacks the o.' The Kalends, being the first of the month, cannot possibly be reconciled with the fifth, except by reading as above.*

Source of Above:
Catiline his conspiracy, by Ben Jonson, edited with introd., notes and glossary
by Lynn Harold Harris
New Haven, Yale University Press, 1916
P. 184.

***

The Regents edition of the play states this in a note:

> [*fifth ... November*] October 27, expressed in Roman style, *ante diem quintum Kalendas Novembres.*

Source: of Above:
Catiline. Ben Jonson. W.F. Bolton and Jane F. Gardner, ed. Lincoln, Nebraska: University of Nebraska Press, 1973.
P. 103.
Apparently, the Regents edition is incorrect because the counting should be inclusive:

Days

While we count the days of the month forwards starting, for example, with the first of April and ending with the 30th, the Romans counted the days backwards. And not just from the end of the month, but from the first quarter and the middle of the month and then from the first day of the next month. So the day we would call the 20th day of January Romans would call the 13th day before the first of February.

That arithmetic only works with inclusive counting — count every day from 20 January to 1 February inclusive.

Source of Above:
"The Roman Calendar"
Paul Lewis
Accessed 13 July 2021.
http://www.web40571.clarahost.co.uk/roman/calhis.htm

For Your Information:

CMHypno (Cynthia), "How and Why the Romans Executed People." Owlcation. 8 June 2016

< https://owlcation.com/humanities/roman-executions-why-the-romans-executed-people >.

This short article does not mention strangling.

For Your Information:

infamost, "Top 10 Horrible Roman Execution Methods." infamost. 28 May 2020

< https://infamost.com/roman-execution-methods/ >.

Note: The readings above are not academic.

The below is from infamost, "Top 10 Horrible Roman Execution Methods":

3. Strangulation

Believe it or not but **spilling blood** inside the Ancient city of Rome (and outside of the arenas) was actually a **big taboo**. Therefore, one of the most common methods of execution was **strangulation**, which conveniently didn't cause a bloody mess.

The condemned would first be **paraded all around the city** before being brought to the **Roman Forum.** There, the executioner would simply strangle the convicted felon to death with a rope.

Sometimes, the prisoner would just be paraded and **taken back to his cell** where he was then **strangled**. This was the case with for example **Vercingetorix**, a captured Gallic tribe leader who was brought to Rome and paraded during **one of 4 of Julius Caesar's triumphs in 46 B.C.**

Source of Above:

infamost, "Top 10 Horrible Roman Execution Methods." infamost. 28 May 2020
     < https://infamost.com/roman-execution-methods/ >.

APPENDIX A: ABOUT THE AUTHOR

It was a dark and stormy night. Suddenly a cry rang out, and on a hot summer night in 1954, Josephine, wife of Carl Bruce, gave birth to a boy — me. Unfortunately, this young married couple allowed Reuben Saturday, Josephine's brother, to name their first-born. Reuben, aka "The Joker," decided that Bruce was a nice name, so he decided to name me Bruce Bruce. I have gone by my middle name — David — ever since.

Being named Bruce David Bruce hasn't been all bad. Bank tellers remember me very quickly, so I don't often have to show an ID. It can be fun in charades, also. When I was a counselor as a teenager at Camp Echoing Hills in Warsaw, Ohio, a fellow counselor gave the signs for "sounds like" and "two words," then she pointed to a bruise on her leg twice. Bruise Bruise? Oh yeah, Bruce Bruce is the answer!

Uncle Reuben, by the way, gave me a haircut when I was in kindergarten. He cut my hair short and shaved a small bald spot on the back of my head. My mother wouldn't let me go to school until the bald spot grew out again.

Of all my brothers and sisters (six in all), I am the only transplant to Athens, Ohio. I was born in Newark, Ohio, and have lived all around Southeastern Ohio. However, I moved to Athens to go to Ohio University and have never left.

At Ohio U, I never could make up my mind whether to major in English or Philosophy, so I got a bachelor's degree with a double major in both areas, then I added a Master of Arts degree in English and a Master of Arts degree in Philosophy. Yes, I have my MAMA degree.

Currently, and for a long time to come (I eat fruits and veggies), I am spending my retirement writing books such as *Nadia Comaneci: Perfect 10*, *The Funniest People in Comedy*, *Homer's* Iliad: *A Retelling in Prose*, and *William Shakespeare's* Hamlet: *A Retelling in Prose*.

By the way, my sister Brenda Kennedy writes romances such as *A New Beginning* and *Shattered Dreams*.

APPENDIX B: SOME BOOKS BY DAVID BRUCE

Retellings of a Classic Work of Literature

Arden of Faversham: *A Retelling*

Ben Jonson's The Alchemist: *A Retelling*

Ben Jonson's The Arraignment, or Poetaster: *A Retelling*

Ben Jonson's Bartholomew Fair: *A Retelling*

Ben Jonson's The Case is Altered: *A Retelling*

Ben Jonson's Catiline's Conspiracy: *A Retelling*

Ben Jonson's The Devil is an Ass: *A Retelling*

Ben Jonson's Epicene: *A Retelling*

Ben Jonson's Every Man in His Humor: *A Retelling*

Ben Jonson's Every Man Out of His Humor: *A Retelling*

Ben Jonson's The Fountain of Self-Love, or Cynthia's Revels: *A Retelling*

Ben Jonson's The Magnetic Lady, or Humors Reconciled: *A Retelling*

Ben Jonson's The New Inn, or The Light Heart: *A Retelling*

Ben Jonson's Sejanus' Fall: *A Retelling*

Ben Jonson's The Staple of News: *A Retelling*

Ben Jonson's A Tale of a Tub: *A Retelling*

Ben Jonson's Volpone, or the Fox: *A Retelling*

Christopher Marlowe's Complete Plays: Retellings

Christopher Marlowe's Dido, Queen of Carthage: *A Retelling*

Christopher Marlowe's Doctor Faustus: *Retellings of the 1604 A-Text and of the 1616 B-Text*

Christopher Marlowe's Edward II: *A Retelling*

Christopher Marlowe's The Massacre at Paris: *A Retelling*

Christopher Marlowe's The Rich Jew of Malta: *A Retelling*

Christopher Marlowe's Tamburlaine, Parts 1 and 2: *Retellings*

Dante's Divine Comedy: *A Retelling in Prose*

Dante's Inferno: *A Retelling in Prose*

Dante's Purgatory: *A Retelling in Prose*

Dante's Paradise: *A Retelling in Prose*

The Famous Victories of Henry V: *A Retelling*

From the Iliad *to the* Odyssey: *A Retelling in Prose of Quintus of Smyrna's* Posthomerica

George Chapman, Ben Jonson, and John Marston's Eastward Ho! *A Retelling*

George Peele's The Arraignment of Paris: *A Retelling*

George Peele's The Battle of Alcazar: *A Retelling*

George's Peele's David and Bathsheba, and the Tragedy of Absalom: *A Retelling*

George Peele's Edward I: *A Retelling*

George Peele's The Old Wives' Tale: *A Retelling*

George-a-Greene: *A Retelling*

The History of King Leir: *A Retelling*

Homer's Iliad: *A Retelling in Prose*

Homer's Odyssey: *A Retelling in Prose*

J.W. Gent.'s The Valiant Scot: *A Retelling*

Jason and the Argonauts: A Retelling in Prose of Apollonius of Rhodes' Argonautica

John Ford: Eight Plays Translated into Modern English

John Ford's The Broken Heart: *A Retelling*

John Ford's The Fancies, Chaste and Noble: *A Retelling*

John Ford's The Lady's Trial: *A Retelling*

John Ford's The Lover's Melancholy: *A Retelling*

John Ford's Love's Sacrifice: *A Retelling*

John Ford's Perkin Warbeck: *A Retelling*

John Ford's The Queen: *A Retelling*

John Ford's 'Tis Pity She's a Whore: *A Retelling*

John Lyly's Campaspe: *A Retelling*

John Lyly's Endymion, The Man in the Moon: *A Retelling*

John Lyly's Galatea: *A Retelling*

John Lyly's Love's Metamorphosis: *A Retelling*

John Lyly's Midas: *A Retelling*

John Lyly's Mother Bombie: *A Retelling*

John Lyly's Sappho and Phao: *A Retelling*

John Lyly's The Woman in the Moon: *A Retelling*

John Webster's The White Devil: *A Retelling*

King Edward III: *A Retelling*

Mankind: *A Medieval Morality Play* (A Retelling)

Margaret Cavendish's The Unnatural Tragedy: *A Retelling*

The Merry Devil of Edmonton: *A Retelling*

The Summoning of Everyman: *A Medieval Morality Play* (A Retelling)

Robert Greene's Friar Bacon and Friar Bungay: *A Retelling*

The Taming of a Shrew: *A Retelling*

Tarlton's Jests: A Retelling

Thomas Middleton's A Chaste Maid in Cheapside: *A Retelling*

Thomas Middleton's Women Beware Women: *A Retelling*

Thomas Middleton and Thomas Dekker's The Roaring Girl: *A Retelling*

Thomas Middleton and William Rowley's The Changeling: *A Retelling*

The Trojan War and Its Aftermath: Four Ancient Epic Poems

Virgil's Aeneid: *A Retelling in Prose*

William Shakespeare's 5 Late Romances: Retellings in Prose

William Shakespeare's 10 Histories: Retellings in Prose

William Shakespeare's 11 Tragedies: Retellings in Prose

William Shakespeare's 12 Comedies: Retellings in Prose

William Shakespeare's 38 Plays: Retellings in Prose
William Shakespeare's 1 Henry IV, aka Henry IV, Part 1: *A Retelling in Prose*
William Shakespeare's 2 Henry IV, aka Henry IV, Part 2: *A Retelling in Prose*
William Shakespeare's 1 Henry VI, aka Henry VI, Part 1: *A Retelling in Prose*
William Shakespeare's 2 Henry VI, aka Henry VI, Part 2: *A Retelling in Prose*
William Shakespeare's 3 Henry VI, aka Henry VI, Part 3: *A Retelling in Prose*
William Shakespeare's All's Well that Ends Well: *A Retelling in Prose*
William Shakespeare's Antony and Cleopatra: *A Retelling in Prose*
William Shakespeare's As You Like It: *A Retelling in Prose*
William Shakespeare's The Comedy of Errors: *A Retelling in Prose*
William Shakespeare's Coriolanus: *A Retelling in Prose*
William Shakespeare's Cymbeline: *A Retelling in Prose*
William Shakespeare's Hamlet: *A Retelling in Prose*
William Shakespeare's Henry V: *A Retelling in Prose*
William Shakespeare's Henry VIII: *A Retelling in Prose*
William Shakespeare's Julius Caesar: *A Retelling in Prose*
William Shakespeare's King John: *A Retelling in Prose*
William Shakespeare's King Lear: *A Retelling in Prose*
William Shakespeare's Love's Labor's Lost: *A Retelling in Prose*
William Shakespeare's Macbeth: *A Retelling in Prose*
William Shakespeare's Measure for Measure: *A Retelling in Prose*
William Shakespeare's The Merchant of Venice: *A Retelling in Prose*
William Shakespeare's The Merry Wives of Windsor: *A Retelling in Prose*
William Shakespeare's A Midsummer Night's Dream: *A Retelling in Prose*
William Shakespeare's Much Ado About Nothing: *A Retelling in Prose*
William Shakespeare's Othello: *A Retelling in Prose*
William Shakespeare's Pericles, Prince of Tyre: *A Retelling in Prose*
William Shakespeare's Richard II: *A Retelling in Prose*
William Shakespeare's Richard III: *A Retelling in Prose*
William Shakespeare's Romeo and Juliet: *A Retelling in Prose*
William Shakespeare's The Taming of the Shrew: *A Retelling in Prose*
William Shakespeare's The Tempest: *A Retelling in Prose*
William Shakespeare's Timon of Athens: *A Retelling in Prose*
William Shakespeare's Titus Andronicus: *A Retelling in Prose*
William Shakespeare's Troilus and Cressida: *A Retelling in Prose*
William Shakespeare's Twelfth Night: *A Retelling in Prose*
William Shakespeare's The Two Gentlemen of Verona: *A Retelling in Prose*
William Shakespeare's The Two Noble Kinsmen: *A Retelling in Prose*
William Shakespeare's The Winter's Tale: *A Retelling in Prose*